THE SHADOW TAKER

Books by Blaine M. Yorgason and/or Brenton G. Yorgason

The Shadow Taker**
The Loftier Way: Tales from the Ancient American Frontier
Brother Brigham's Gold
Ride the Laughing Wind
The Miracle
Chester, I Love You
Double Exposure
Seeker of the Gentle Heart
The Krystal Promise
A Town Called Charity and Other Stories About Decisions
The Bishop's Horse Race
The Courage Covenant (Massacre at Salt Creek)
Windwalker (movie version—out of print)
The Windwalker
Others
Charlie's Monument
From First Date to Chosen Mate
Tall Timber (out of print)
Miracles and the Latter-day Saint Teenager (out of print)
From Two to One*
From This Day Forth*
Creating a Celestial Marriage (textbook)*
Marriage and Family Stewardships (textbook)*

Tapes

Caring and Sharing (Blaine M. Yorgason—two taped talks)
Things Most Plain and Precious (Brenton G. Yorgason—two taped talks)
The Joyous Way (Blaine & Brenton Yorgason—two taped talks)
The Miracle (dramatized tape of book)
Charlie's Monument (taped reading of book)
The Bishop's Horse Race (taped reading of book)

*Coauthored with Wesley R. Burr and Terry R. Baker
**Coauthored with Carl J. Eaton

THE SHADOW TAKER

Blaine M. Yorgason
with
Carl J. Eaton

Deseret Book Company
Salt Lake City, Utah

This book is a work of fiction. With the exception of historical information about the Hole-in-the-Rock pioneers, names, characters, places, and incidents either are the product of the author's imagination or are used fictitiously, and any resemblance to actual persons, living or dead; organizations; events; or locales is entirely coincidental.

First printing, November 1985

Library of Congress Cataloging-in-Publication Data

Yorgason, Blaine M., 1942–
    The shadow taker.

    I. Eaton, Carl J.   II. Title.
PS3575.O57S46 1985   813'.54   85-20593
ISBN 0-87579-018-6

For Max and Mava

Contents

The Driver

Water!

The driver of the old jeep needed water, and before long he was going to need it badly. In the scorching July heat his body was losing moisture rapidly, and he knew that soon such a loss would begin to affect his thinking. The driver understood the danger of that, understood too that it would take him at least until sundown to reach the water at Mormon Wells in Wilson Canyon. The chances were that he would make it, but the old jeep could have more problems. If it did, he would be in trouble. Yet even that thought made the driver grin humorlessly.

Yesterday the jeep's radiator had sprung a leak. He had not worried, however, for he carried almost six gallons of water with him and could replenish it at Lake Canyon. And so he had kept the radiator filled and had used almost half his water doing so. But then last evening he had found the stream in Lake Canyon dry, something he had never before known to happen, and so he had started to conserve. He had dug several holes in the sand of the stream bed to gather seepage, had taken a very small drink and gone to sleep, and this morning had found his holes still dry.

But even then he hadn't really worried. He still had a little over two gallons in his container and almost a gallon in an old milk jug in the back of the jeep, and it wasn't any big drive to Mormon Wells. In fact, because the distance was so short and because he felt such a desire to conquer this strange land of heat and wind and rock, he had bypassed the wells and had gone north and around to Cottonwood Canyon by a route he had discovered the year before. He shouldn't have done it—he knew that, but his desire to prove his own strength was incredible. And his task would have been fairly easy, too, if only he'd been more careful. He had tipped over his five-gallon water container as he had climbed out of his jeep to do a little hiking at Cottonwood Canyon. But in his haste he hadn't even noticed. His two gallons had leaked through the loosely tightened lid and seeped into the hot sand, and now, except for the milk jug, he was without water.

Probably served him right, he thought grimly. Such carelessness deserved at least a little suffering. In fact, maybe the Lord was punishing him for something or other. He grinned wryly at the thought, his dry lips cracked and split with the grin, and as he wiped away a tiny fleck of blood he realized that he was drier than he had supposed.

Challenges. He had always believed that happiness came from facing challenges. He was facing a real one now, and he felt himself quickening to the exhilaration of it. He would make it, and then he would truly be ready.

In compound four-wheel drive the old jeep inched up the tortuous slick-rock hummock, each inch a victory over gravity and the intense heat, each

2

foot a foot closer to the water the driver so desperately needed for his jeep and for himself.

Tall, slim, athletic looking, and yet dignified even in his rough desert garb, the driver was in his late thirties. His finely chiseled features were framed by thick, dark hair that held only a touch of gray. His expression was usually pleasant, and most who knew him considered him one of the best-looking men they had ever known. He knew that, of course, and was intelligent enough to acknowledge it without being puffed up by it. After all, his looks were one of his more significant assets, and they had certainly contributed in at least some way to the great string of successes he had enjoyed.

Now he maneuvered the wheel expertly and leaned forward as if to aid his vehicle up the incredibly steep slope, his personal features the furthest thing from his mind. Water was what he thought of. Water and surviving. In all conditions, he was best at surviving.

Suddenly the angle of pitch steepened, the balding tires on the jeep spun momentarily, and the driver's grin faded. Quickly he hit the clutch, stomped on the accelerator, and eased back his foot to engage the gears. Finally, with gunned throttle, the vehicle lurched over the top of the hill and bounced crazily across the rock toward the next descent.

The driver, grinning again, glanced quickly into the heat-warped distance. Off to the north and west rose the Henry Mountains, while to the south and east the blue bulk of Navajo Mountain jutted upward off the abrupt end of the Kaiparowits Plateau. Between them, where he ground his way slowly along, was the path followed by the old Hole-in-the-Rock pioneers, and once again, as he had on at least

3

a half-dozen other occasions, he was following and exploring their primitive trail.

Again he licked his burning lips and thought of water. Why, why had he bypassed Wilson Canyon and its deep rock tanks? Sometimes his own arrogance truly frightened him. When he should have been taking care of himself and his jeep, he had instead gone foolishly scouting, looking for better ways those crazy old pioneers could have taken.

He had driven that day through the breaks and across the top of Wilson or Gray Mesa to the north, going almost to the Rincon in his search. He had also been down in Iceberg Canyon, but that tortuous, twisting gash in the rock had proven one of the most difficult hikes, if also one of the shortest, he had ever taken.

South of the old trail was more of Wilson Mesa, completely surrounded by the writhing course of the San Juan River that had now become an arm of Lake Powell. He had found stretches where the old pioneers might have done better, had they been there. But they had come up out of Cottonwood Canyon the only way they could have, and they had been searching for the most direct route to Montezuma Fort. Thus they had taken the course they had. Only it was the craziest route he or anyone else had ever seen. In places it looked as though they had deliberately chosen the most difficult, the most dangerous, the most ridiculous route for their wagons. And try as he would, the driver could not understand that.

Why had they come this way at all? Why had they given almost a year of their lives to blasting and chipping a useless road through a wilderness of rock called the San Juan Desert? And more than why, the driver always found himself wondering how. How had they accomplished such a feat and remained alive to tell of it? The terrain was incredibly steep, amazingly treacherous, constantly deceptive. It was country where one watched closely where he placed each foot, for a single misstep might easily mean death. It was a country where great challenges and fearful dangers were the results of every decision made.

Still, it was a lovely land, lovely and dry and lonely. He loved it, but he knew that few others felt the same. Men and women had been there with him, people who hated the desert, the seemingly never-ending rock, the incredible heat, and the almost complete absence of life. Of course, there were the crows, the buzzards, the eagles, the rodents, and the occasional rattlesnakes, but these were not appreciated by most people and were certainly not considered as life. So now when the driver came into the land, he usually came alone, content with the company of his own thoughts, his own appreciation for the majesty of the San Juan slick-rock wilderness.

Again the jeep lurched as the front wheels dropped into a sixteen-inch seam in the rock. Again the driver throttled forward, and with a responding surge of power the vehicle lunged upward, dragging its rear wheels through the seam and up after it. Without thought the driver eased off the gas, wiped his brow with the back of his long-sleeved shirt, and spun the steering wheel to the left to avoid an even deeper seam in the time-frozen old sand dune.

Time. How slowly it seemed to pass, and how rapidly it actually flew by. Once the slick-rock had been sand; now it was stone. Once the sand had been stirred up and surrounded by water; now there was only a desert of twisted sedimentary rock with little water anywhere. So much time it had taken, and yet it was already past, and he was there to see the results.

And it was the same with his own life, he reflected. Once he had thought he would always be young, but now he could actually see age creeping in upon him. Each day went by so quickly that the weeks were a blur, and he could hardly imagine where the years since his high-school days had gone. Time was simply moving faster.

For instance, just a few days before, his trip into the desert had loomed indefinitely ahead, a whole unending week of solitary pleasure. Now it was already Thursday afternoon. He had been exploring the old Hole-in-the-Rock trail from San Juan Hill backward for almost the entire week, and after this one last night under the stars at Mormon Wells, he would be on his way home—at least he would be if he could get to water.

Home! As his thoughts turned there, his pulse quickened. Jeannie, his wife, would be waiting there, his companion of almost twenty years; and his children would be there too, also waiting, though neither of them would have been as aware of his absence as had his wife. Of course that was to be expected, for the children were rapidly maturing, and their lives should no longer center in their home. But his wife would have missed him, and he looked forward to being with her again.

Jan and Bryan, his children. He and Jeannie had done their best to teach them and to provide good opportunities for them, and it had paid off. They were good kids. And actually, he admitted to himself, his children's goodness was due much more to his wife's teachings and example than to his. She was one of the finest people he had ever known, and he felt blessed to be married to her.

Of course *he* wasn't exactly evil, either. After all,

he had been successful in his insurance business and so had been able to give his family much more than the necessities of life. He was basically a kind man and tried most of the time to be a patient and loving father. And, perhaps most importantly, he had been involved in the Church ever since the days of his mission. He felt that he was pretty good about keeping most of the commandments, and he was trying to keep the others. And he had always accepted the callings that had come his way.

Licking his lips to ease the pain brought on by the burning sun, the driver shifted the jeep down to crawl through a winding wash that cut up through the ragged edge of Gray Mesa. Reflexively he wiped his brow and thought of the 120-degree heat, and again he squinted into the distance. The land *was* lovely, but it could be so hostile, so dangerous. Still, that was part of his fascination for it, part of the reason why he came again and again into its solitary vastness. His coming was a challenge, an ancient rite wherein he proved over and over his own strength as he battled, and ultimately overcame, the silently waiting land where the old Hole-in-the-Rock pioneers had once trod their foolish but amazing way.

Those old pioneers had certainly been dedicated, his mind told him. Anyone who had ever crossed this slick-rock wilderness had to admit at least that much about them. Dedicated, but completely beyond his understanding.

Hole-in-the-Rock. He had never been to that two-thousand-foot slit in the cliff above where the Colorado had now become Lake Powell, but he had seen pictures of it and had even seen it from the hazy distance of Cottonwood Canyon, and he felt that the people must have been crazy to have gone down it. They had surely been crazy to have come

7

up out of Cottonwood Canyon the way they had come, for that was the trail he now followed, and it was indeed a trail of insanity.

Why and how a group of families, with eighty-three wagons and over a thousand head of stock, would willingly go through such a hellish experience was simply beyond his understanding.

Of course, for him, in his jeep, it was different. He risked only himself, and the jeep made it hardly any risk at all. He could go, in hours, to places where they had spent days and even weeks getting to. So why and how had they done such a thing?

8

In the past few years the driver had climbed and descended the old trail in every place it could be found. He had placed his fingers in the small holes made by hand-held drills and hand-wielded single-jacks; he had stepped in tiny terraces chiseled out of the rock to hold sand and give footing to man and beast; he had strained to lift boulders that made up the lower side of narrow, cliff-hanging roads, rocks that were stacked eight, ten, twelve feet high, and that were, even today, almost impossible for a man to lift.

No, to say he did not understand those old pioneers was probably a misstatement. Actually, he felt that he did understand them, and he considered them all to have been either crazy or very stupid.

But in a way he envied them, envied what they had been able to accomplish. How he would have liked to have lived back then when he could have pitted his strength against the land as they had. How he would have loved to be part of what they had done, to be part of the strong memories they had left behind. Yet deep down he knew that his envy of their achievement was foolish. He was just as dedicated as any of them had been, just as strong.

Only his strength had to be pitted against the hard facts of modern economic life, and that was probably even tougher than the desert.

No, those Hole-in-the-Rock pioneers had lived in a different world when situations had been less, well, less ambiguous. You either took one path or you took another, and there were no in-betweens. Thus it had been easier for them to determine right from wrong. The driver was sure of that.

Now, though he still believed in the same principles of the gospel that had motivated those old Mormon settlers, the driver knew that life had become harder. Thus he was forced to live the gospel in a different way, under a different set of rules.

For instance, in the early days of the Church many of the Saints had used alcohol and tobacco even after the Word of Wisdom had been given. Now that had changed, and he wouldn't even have considered drinking socially or smoking. By the same token, what had been either truth or dishonesty back in the days of the pioneers had now become a thousand varied shades of whatever a person chose to call what he was doing. All the rules had changed, the issues were clouded, and a man was forced to say whatever he had to say in order to survive.

Nor was such a person bad. He was simply smart, and how could being smart earn anything from God but blessings? After all, didn't the scriptures say that whatsoever degree of intelligence a man attained in this life would rise with him? Smart was intelligent; intelligent was smart. That being the case, his survival philosophy of life *had* to be the right way to live.

And that, truthfully, was why he was out in the desert again now. Of course, he was ritually celebrating the new position he had just landed. But

9

more than that, he was gathering his strength, pitting himself once more against the land that the old pioneers had conquered, reminding himself of who he really was so that he could go forth as he had in the past and continue to set the insurance world on fire.

Nor was there really any doubt in his mind about his ability to do so. He had proven himself again and again as he had risen in the industry. He was a winner, a driver, and those qualities were as obvious to him as they were to anyone else. Some people had it, others didn't, and he was fortunate enough to be one of those who did.

With a sudden ache in his heart, the driver thought of his friend Homer Bean, his associate and his only competitor for the position he had just landed. He liked Homer, always had, and he felt real sorrow for the man. It wasn't that Homer was bad; in fact, he wasn't. The trouble was that he was a loser, a non-competitor in the game of life.

Homer was overweight and hadn't really taken care of himself. He didn't dress well, and, in fact, most of the time he looked as if he had just walked out of the bargain basement of a thrift store.

The man had other problems, too, but the main barrier in his road to success was his timidity. He wasn't aggressive, he wasn't assertive, he wasn't decisive, and he certainly didn't create or take advantage of the opportunities that came so naturally to those who wanted to grow.

For example, both he and Homer had been in college together, studying business in the same classes. They had both done reasonably well, and at the end of that school year he had landed a summer job with AMPAX Insurance. Homer hadn't been able to find work, so the driver had talked to his boss, and Homer had been hired.

Both had sold policies, and both had realized that they wanted to remain in the insurance industry from then on. But where he had dropped out of school, focused on his career, and so had moved steadily forward, Homer had gone back to school and had fiddled along as a part-time salesman for the next several years, never really focusing on his career advancement.

Of course Homer now had a degree, but so what? In all that time he should have had two or three. Besides, his sales figures were only average, so the degree hadn't helped at all where it really counted. And though he had somehow been given a manager's slot, his office was at best a mediocre office in a mediocre location with even more mediocre sales figures. Even worse, Homer always picked up the poorest salesmen, more losers whom the driver himself had tried out and eliminated. Of course, those sorry souls always managed to sell one or two policies a month for Homer, but considering all the time he gave them in training, they ought to have been able to sell circles around themselves.

Why, he even shared his commissions and clients with the slowest of his men, and the driver had never been able to convince Homer that doing such things was against all the principles of sound business management.

What really got to the driver, however, was Homer's timidity in closing his own sales. He was a quiet man, and he never really asserted himself anywhere. But besides that he was mentally soft; he was forever pulling back because he felt sorry for the client. Occasionally he even gave up his commissions so that his clients could afford a better policy, and doing that was business suicide.

Instead, the driver felt, Homer should have been more tough-minded, more creative, more willing to push the client and mold him to the policy he was offering. Every good salesman knew that people could afford exactly what they wanted to afford, and insurance clients were no different. All an agent had to do was convince the client that he couldn't live without the policy, and then trim and cut the coverage so that the client could see the good deal he was getting. Then the sale would be closed.

But Homer couldn't do that, never had and probably never would. He simply let his emotions get in the way of his career, both in the hiring of poor salesmen and in the easing off on clients. He had no moxie, no charisma, and so he was a poor salesman.

The driver knew the problems such a personality created, knew that an insurance executive was always chosen because of his charisma and his production figures, and so he could hardly understand how Homer had managed to advance at all. Only somehow the poor man had, bumbling and struggling daily in his grinding climb upward. Yet even more amazing to the driver was the fact that somehow Homer had come, after all these years, nose to nose with him, vying for the position of regional representative of AMPAX Insurance.

The decision of those above the driver to even consider a person such as Homer Bean was completely beyond the driver's understanding. Why, under Homer's direction the entire region would have gone to pot. There were no two ways about it. Yet for some obscure reason the president of AMPAX had narrowed the field of possible regional representatives from thirty to twelve, from twelve to six, and from six to two—himself and, incredibly, Homer Bean.

When he had learned that the selected candidates had been reduced to himself and poor old

Homer, the driver had not known whether to laugh or cry. Homer was such a sorry figure that he ached for him. Why put the poor guy through the misery of falsely expecting such a position? It was not fair. One day, the driver vowed, he himself would head the company, and then such decisions, decisions that only hurt people like Homer and his ridiculous corps of salesmen, would never be made again.

And as always, for he had a feel for such things, the driver had been right about himself and Homer Bean. He had been given the job, and in the final analysis, Homer had hardly even been considered.

So now he was here in the desert celebrating and preparing himself for his new position while Homer, no doubt, was home trying to tell Ann, his wife, why they would always live in poverty.

Suddenly the driver smelled steam, so he pulled to a stop where the land dipped and he could gaze out over the edge of Gray Mesa. A wisp of water vapor was coming from the front of the jeep, so the driver lifted the hood and waited while things cooled a little.

With his hand the driver felt the radiator and the engine. Both were too hot to touch. That was typical of an engine, but he didn't think a radiator should be so hot. He waited awhile longer and then gingerly opened the radiator. As far as he could tell, it was as dry as a bone. It needed water, but he hoped it would not need more than two quarts.

Reluctantly he picked up the milk jug, sloshed his last bit of water around, and fought down his desire for a drink. With a wry grin he poked his finger into the water, licked it, forced himself to laugh at his own silliness, and then carefully poured his last couple of quarts of water into the radiator. That done, he lifted the empty jug and let what drops were left trickle into his mouth.

13

Good, but not anywhere near enough. Yet it was his last, and now he had to get to Mormon Wells with what was in the radiator. It would be close, but he could do it if he was careful, careful and very lucky.

Tossing the jug back into the jeep, the driver stretched, wiped his lips, and looked around. It was steep where the earth dropped off below him. The wind and the silence whipped at him, and the deep blue of Lake Powell, spread out far below in the Great Bend of the San Juan, seemed somehow out of place.

"Like Homer," the driver said ruefully, speaking aloud into the wind. "Always out of place. How I wish there were some way I could help him!"

For another moment the driver gazed at the distant azure of the lake, thinking then of all the water that was so far below him. More miles of shore than the entire western coast of the United States, he had been told. Now he wished he were swimming in it, or boating on it, or pouring gallons of it into the worn-out radiator of his overheated jeep. The water looked so cool, so delicious!

Licking his dry lips again, the driver checked the radiator and decided that it had cooled enough, closed the hood, started the jeep, shifted up, and for perhaps five minutes flew across the mesa at speeds approaching thirty miles an hour. But then the land broke apart into gullies and cracks, and again he was forced to shift down into compound low.

Beneath his hands the steering wheel pulled and twisted as the jeep ground its way across the tortuous terrain, and again and again the driver shifted the gears and manipulated his vehicle as he felt with the tires for a roadway. He was the jeep now, and the jeep seemed merely an extension of himself. Thus he reached out, feeling his way carefully but with great confidence across the slick-rock desert.

Just driving his old jeep was hard work, hard and dangerous. And beyond the hazards of driving, the hostile land lay waiting, seeming almost ready to pounce and destroy.

The driver thought again of the old pioneers who had come across the land, and again he wondered about them. They had had a choice of going either to the north or to the south and so skirting this tortured country, and so of taking six weeks to get to Montezuma Creek. Yet that had seemed too long a time to them, so they had elected to take a shortcut straight through, a shortcut that turned out to be an almost seven-month trek through some of the roughest country on the face of the earth.

Yet those people had unwittingly provided him with a focal point, a difficult, strenuous goal that would enable him to focus his drive, his energies, his ambition.

Only now, in this heat with no water and his old jeep acting up, the driver found himself wondering—

Again he wiped the sweat from his forehead and then tugged his hat lower against the glare of the sun. Again he licked his parchment-dry lips, and again he squinted out across the slick-rock.

"Blasted heat," he muttered. "Why does it have to be so miserably hot? I can take almost anything, but with no water this heat, this . . ."

Suddenly incredibly thirsty, the driver reached for his empty plastic milk jug, tilted it, and waited, hoping for another single last drop. None came, and so with a growl of disgust he tossed the jug behind him again.

He glanced once more at the sun, and for the hundredth time he thought of the tanks at Mormon Wells below the Chute in Wilson Canyon. In his mind he could see and even taste the water that filled the huge rock holes. He felt his mouth aching with even greater thirst, and with all his heart he wished he were already there.

But he would be. Soon he would be, and then all would be well.

16

The Old Man

The sun had finally dropped behind the distant Kaiparowits Plateau when the steaming jeep topped the lip of the steep descent and lurched downward into the narrow defile known as Wilson Canyon. Through burning eyes the driver glanced around, saw no sign of the water anywhere, and suddenly feared that the tanks he had so longed to reach might be empty.

When the Hole-in-the-Rock scouts had discovered these tanks, there had been water in them, plenty of it. But it had been winter then, not so hot, and so the tanks had not seemed so precious as they did now to him. Still, in a land so infernal and so desolate, tanks of water were a godsend wherever they were. And the land he crossed was truly infernal, truly desolate.

At the bottom of the slick-rock descent, the driver paused for a moment to gaze toward the opposite slope and up the incredibly steep defile the old pioneers had called the Chute and up which they had hauled their wagons when they had left Mormon Wells. He thought for a moment of driving up it in the morning.

Of course it was steep, but he had driven up it before. What made it interesting was that the old Hole-in-the-Rock folks had declared that the Lord had prepared that defile expressly for their wagons to climb out through. The driver always grinned at that thought. If it were true, then the Lord must have been a tolerably poor engineer. Had the driver created the Chute instead of the Lord, he'd have lessened the grade and probably made it smoother while he was at it.

The driver grunted again at the thought of folks believing such nonsense, turned up an apparently dead-end draw, pulled onto a sandy bench, and stopped. In the sudden stillness he gazed upward into the rocks, and only after a long moment did the whisper of the wind find its way past the hissing of the radiator and into his consciousness.

He loved the wind. He loved the way it moaned across the rocks, sang through the rare junipers that grew here and there, and whispered as it lifted the dry June-grass to dance. Now for a moment he listened to its soft music, and then with a sigh he reached for his empty jug, swung out the open side of the jeep, and began to climb.

The first tanks he came to were empty of all but dry sand and gravel, but the driver climbed on, forcing himself to be confident, and was soon rewarded with the sight of water. The first three holes were small and shallow, but just beyond them were two others, larger and much deeper.

Lying down on the rock near the deepest of the tanks, he pushed back the scum and watched as the pollywogs wriggled away. Then joyfully he scooped the water out and splashed it across his face and behind his neck. That done, he drank thirstily, thinking all the while of how reluctant his wife would be to taste the same cool water, and of how much she would be missing by not doing so. There was no better water anywhere, yet only the truly thirsty could appreciate it.

Finished, the driver filled his jug, drank again, and then like a child jumped into the tank. The water felt cool and good as he went under. He came up splashing and blowing water, feeling the coolness seeping into his body, and then he ducked under again. At last he simply sat with the water just under his chin, watched the tank slowly clear, and grinned that such a wonderful supply of good water could be found in such a forsaken stretch of sandstone. Yet that was only one of the mysteries of the desert, and he knew it.

Off to the south, where there was no water at all, there was a cave that was used occasionally by cowboys as a winter line camp. Yet in the rock of that cave were petroglyphs, rock art showing that the ancient Anasazi had been there. Then too there was a Spanish cross carved deeply into the stone, and that cross had been the basis of someone's decision to call the place Escalante's Cave. Whether or not Escalante had ever been there no one knew, but some old Spanish padre, probably out hunting gold, had spent time there, that was certain.

There were other mysteries too, stone dwellings of the old Indians that had been abandoned almost in the middle of a meal so many centuries before; a Spanish stone fort on the bluff above the east fork of Lake Creek that seemed to guard nothing; an abandoned army half-track with air still in its front tires; and so on. He could never solve those mysteries, of course, but that was one of the reasons why he loved the desert. He thrived on challenge, and the idea of understanding those things, as well as understanding the motives and accomplishments of the old pioneers who had blazed a trail across this land, was one of the greatest challenges he had ever faced.

At last the driver climbed from the tank and stood to stretch and dry off, thinking as he did so of where would be the best place to camp.

And that was when he first smelled the smoke.

The odor was a combination of roasting meat and cedar or juniper, but that was not so important. What troubled the driver was that he had come to the tanks the only way he knew of to get there, and there had been no other tracks in the sand. Nor for that matter had he seen any sign of the fire he now smelled.

Carefully he placed his jug of water down, sniffed the air again, and then quietly climbed the rock beyond the tank where he had drunk.

Easing his head above the shelf of sandstone so that he might see without being seen, he was surprised to discover an old man—a Navajo, he guessed—seated at a small fire.

Quickly the driver looked around for other people or signs that other people were near. But as far as he could tell, the old man was alone.

"Ya-ta-he," the driver said softly in greeting, using one of the few Navajo words he knew and hoping that his sudden appearance wouldn't frighten the old man.

But it didn't, for the man simply lifted his head, gazed at the driver for a moment, and then motioned for him to come forward and sit.

And, after a moment's hesitation, the driver complied.

For a time the two men sat in silence, neither of them moving or speaking. This did not bother the driver, for he knew it was customary. Yet all the while his eyes were busy, and it wasn't long before a question or two began to form in his mind.

Try as he would, he could not see clearly the old man's face, and he did not understand why. The fire was distinct, the leg of mutton roasting above it was distinct, and the knife placed in the sand before him for the cutting of the meat was distinct. Therefore the driver found himself dealing with the uncanny impression that he was being hidden from. And, strangely, he felt that he had been expected, even waited for, by the old Indian.

For long minutes they silently waited, the driver feeling more and more nervous and more and more determined not to show his nervousness. Still the old man sat without moving, not even seeming to breathe. It was uncanny how he was just . . . well, just *there,* immovable, unseeable, and the more the driver thought about it, the more he wished he had not come forward and seated himself.

He stared again into the shadow that was before him, and suddenly his decision was made. If the old man had not moved within the next sixty seconds, he would get up and leave. He waited, nothing happened, and he was just ready to stand up when at last the old man spoke.

"You may cut the meat now," he said quietly and in perfect English.

Startled, the driver stared at the obscured form, but then he reached down for the knife, feeling almost that he had no choice but to do as the old man had told him.

Not taking his eyes off the old man, he sliced a strip of mutton from the roasted leg and held it out across the fire. With a nod the Indian took it and silently began to chew. The driver watched, wondering that he still could not see the man's face, and wondering too that the shadow beneath the old man's black, high-crowned, silver-conchoed hat could be so deep. Finally, however, he sliced a strip for himself, and soon he too was enjoying the delicious taste of the meat.

Later, when he had finished and was wishing for another drink and wondering why he had left his jug of water down by the tank, the old man suddenly signaled with his hand. Slowly the driver looked down where the man had motioned, and the hair on the back of his neck rose as he saw a clay dipper sitting in the sand at his feet, filled to the brim with clear water.

"How . . . ?" he whispered almost fearfully, wondering what sort of witchcraft the old man was using against him.

"Does not every man wish to finish a good meal with a sweet drink?" the old man asked without waiting for the driver to finish his question. "Of course. Now partake, and afterward perhaps there will be a little medicine made between the two of us."

Hesitantly the driver lifted the dipper to his mouth, noticed through the water the black-on-white markings of the ancient Anasazi pottery, wondered that this piece could be in such fine condition, and wondered then where the old man had found it. In this area there were no ruins that he knew of, and in the ruins farther east all the perfect artifacts had been gathered up. Yet here this piece was, in the old man's possession, and the driver found himself speculating on the source of the piece and wondering whether or not he could talk the old man into revealing that source to him.

And then he tasted the water.

Water? It was more like sweet juice, or the finest, most thirst-quenching, coolest liquid he had ever tasted. The old man must have found a tank higher up, the driver instantly decided, one not so polluted with tadpoles and other wildlife.

22

The driver drank greedily until the dipper was almost empty, set it down carefully so that he could finish it later, and suddenly remembered the old man's statement about making medicine, an antiquated Indian term for talking or discussing.

"Well," he said casually as he leaned his elbow back upon the sand, "you mentioned making medicine. What would you like to discuss?"

"Your shadow."

"Excuse me?"

The old man seemed to smile patiently, and then he explained. "I would like to discuss your shadow, and what my possession of it will mean to you."

Now the driver grinned, for at last he understood. The old man had gone over the edge—he was insane. And he had been left in this place by his people to die. They sometimes still did that, he knew, and barbaric though it seemed, it was usually the best answer.

For an instant he was tempted to get up, head for his jeep, and leave. But he was curious and sensed that the old man was harmless, and so he stayed.

"You seem to have the best of me," he said softly, playing with the old man and saving the ridiculous issue of his shadow until last. "A little while ago I had the feeling that I was expected, yet I did not even intend to come here. Nor would I have if I had not had a little accident. Did you hear my jeep?"

"Of course," the old man replied from the darkness that seemed to cover his face, "but before that I knew too. I heard the thirsty rock lap up the last of the water you spilled. I saw you digging in the dry sand for water last evening. And I knew that you knew of this place. Thus here I came to wait."

Momentarily the driver forgot his certainty that

the old man was insane. "You were there on the mesa where I spilled the water?" he questioned incredulously. "You were . . . you were in Lake Canyon? But . . . but that's impossible! I was alone! Besides that, all day and almost all week I have been back and forth on this mesa, and during that time there has been no other living thing in sight. I know, for I notice such things."

"Perhaps you do," the old man conceded. "But then I *did* know of your spilled water and the empty seep holes, didn't I?"

The driver reluctantly agreed that he had. "But then you people have some interesting powers," he added sarcastically, putting the old man easily back into his place. "Powers given you from the dark side of eternity, I would imagine. Nevertheless, for the time being I will play your silly game. How did you know?"

The old man smiled, or at least the driver had the feeling that he was smiling. Actually he couldn't tell, for the darkness on the old man's face had not altered at all.

"There are ways and then there are ways," the old man answered. "You are setting yours as if in stone, just as the old pioneers did with their road, and so I have no difficulty keeping ahead of you."

The driver stared, wishing with all his heart that he could see into that shadow, thinking that perhaps within it he might see the solution to the old fool's crazy riddles. Yet darkness was falling and here and there a star shone already, and so the gloom about the old man was deeper than ever. But his form was not in gloom, and suddenly, for the second time since he had sat down before the fire, the driver became aware of the old man's clothing.

"No!" his mind screamed while his skin crawled with a nameless dread. "No, it can't be!"

24

Only it was, for what at first had seemed a dirty shirt and trousers were now obviously skins, old, tanned, but seemingly clean, and wrapped around the old man's body rather than sewn. Nor did he wear shoes or moccasins, but sandals made of grass or some other fibrous material. His hat, now that the driver looked at it more closely, wasn't wrapped with silver conchos either, but was only another piece of skin, hardened and stretched and made especially for sheltering the face from the sun. None of this was Navajo, and the driver wondered that he had ever thought it might be so in the first place.

25

Yet deep down he did not wonder, for he knew. He *had* seen those Navajo things. He had! It was just that—

Water! That had to be it. He had been without water for too long. His system was still trying to recover, and his mind was simply playing tricks on him.

"What did you mean?" he suddenly asked, trying to clear the cobwebs from his thinking. "What am I setting as if in stone? And if you don't mind my asking, who are you, and how the deuce did you get here?"

The old man did not answer. The darkness deepened, and the flames licked at two small limbs that lay across their hungry mouths. The stars grew more bright above them, and the driver grew more and more nervous.

Finally the old man took up the dipper and spilled a little water on the fire, and a gust of wind whipped out of nowhere and took the burst of steam and smoke away into the darkness. And still the driver could not see the old man's face, his eyes.

"Where I come from," the driver declared with exasperation, "a man who ignores another is called rude. Old man, I appreciate the meal and the drink, but I've asked you some questions, and I think I deserve some answers."

"As with ways," the old man finally responded, "there are answers and then there are answers. Which would you prefer?"

"What? I don't understand."

"Your answer. Would you rather hear what would make you most comfortable, my friend, or would you rather hear—"

"The truth!" the driver interrupted. Then, with all the authority he could muster thrown into his voice, the driver growled ahead. "Old man, forget the riddles and the nonsense! I want the absolute truth from you, and I want it now. Tell me what's going on!"

The old man continued to stare out of the darkness under his hat, but at last with a soft voice he carefully answered.

"Very well, the truth, for that is what I prefer always to speak. I came to this place by a trail only I can take, and my name matters not at all. What does matter is that I am called, among other things, Taker of Shadows, and this day you have given me yours."

"Wh-what?"

"Your shadow. As I declared to you before, this day you have given it to me, and that will have great significance to you."

"Don't be ridiculous," the driver muttered scornfully. And he *was* scornful. Only, deep within his soul he was worried, and for the life of him he couldn't understand why. After all, the old man had obviously lost his mind, and so the silly dialogue was pointless. Yet still the driver had the most unpleasant feeling, the most nervous sensation he had ever felt. All was not well, for the old man seemed too sincere, too knowing. Something was not right, and the longer he stayed around the old man, the worse things would get.

"No one can take a shadow!" he declared abruptly. "Shadows are . . . well . . . they are just untakable."

"Not so," the old man said quietly. "I have yours, for that is my mission and my errand, to gather in the shadows of men and women such as you."

"That's garbage!" the driver scorned, and with a lunge he rose to his feet to leave. Only—

He was still seated. The fire was still licking at the two sticks, the stars were just as bright as they had been moments before, the wind still blew, and the insects of the night still chirped and sang. And the old man was still sitting before him, still holding onto the ancient Anasazi dipper that was somehow still full of water.

Angrily the driver rose once again, intent upon getting to his jeep and then getting out of the narrow canyon. Only—

Again he was still seated. The fire was still licking at the two sticks, the stars were just as bright above him, the wind still blew, and the insects of the night still chirped and sang. And the old man remained sitting before him, still in shadow, still holding the dipper quietly in his hand.

More frightened than he wanted to admit, the driver almost frantically tried again to stand up and then realized with a sickening feeling that he was still exactly as he had been before.

"All right," he snarled, suddenly certain that he knew what had happened to him. "What did you put into that water?"

"Nothing," the old man responded kindly. "Whatever was in it was put there by yourself."

"Don't lie to me, old man. With your evil tricks

27

you've done something to me, and it had to be either the water or the meat."

"I did nothing," the old man responded. "The meat was sweet because you expected it to be so, and the water was delicious for the same reason."

"What are you talking about?"

"Look, and you shall see."

Carefully the driver lowered his eyes, and as he saw the rotted, putrifying mutton hanging in decaying tatters above the fire, as he saw the crawling green filth in the bottom of the ancient broken dipper, the bile rose in his throat and he turned to the side and retched.

28

"H-how?" he gasped when at last he had regained his composure. "How . . . how . . . ?"

"Your shadow," the old man answered easily. "As I told you, none of this could happen, not until you had given me your shadow. You expect filth and corruption to be sweet, and so I allow the Evil One to see that it is, at least for as long as the time you are allotted before your learning begins."

"Oh come on," the driver said. "What have you used? Drugs? Peyote?"

The old man chuckled. "I suppose you might call it that," he laughed quietly. "Your choice of living habits *could* be called drugs, for they have certainly numbed you to other things. But no, my friend, it was not I who administered your attitudes to you. I cannot do that. It was you, and you alone. However, now that you have chosen them and set your way as if in the stone of this land, I have full power over you."

"Listen," the driver growled, letting anger fill his voice exactly as he did when he was forcing his will upon a stubborn or stupid client, "I'm warning you, old man! You've gone too far. This time you've fooled around with the wrong hombre. When I get back I'll turn you in so fast your head will spin."

"There is no point in arguing or threatening," the old man replied quietly. "The deed is done. I have power over you, and I have it only because you have given me your shadow. Now, for as long as it takes, I will stay with you while you learn."

Incredulous, the driver stared into the darkness that was the old man. This was crazy, all of it. He wasn't there at Mormon Wells; he hadn't eaten that putrified flesh nor drunk that horrid water. In fact, he wasn't having this conversation at all. Instead, he was out on the mesa in his jeep. It was still hot daylight, and he was hallucinating from the heat and the dryness that had taken his mind.

That was right. It was like a mirage, and all he had to do was . . . was . . . Well, all he had to do was prove that it was so, pull himself together. Then he could be on his way.

The fire! Now, that would be a way to prove it. Real as it looked and felt, the fire could be no more a part of reality than any of the rest of the circumstances in which he seemed to be. Thus, if he could thrust his hand into the flames and the coals, there would be no pain, no burning, and the knowledge of that would bring him to himself. Then he could get on with finding Mormon Wells and getting the water he so desperately needed. It was so, and suddenly, deep within himself, he knew it!

Quickly, then, the driver reached forward and thrust his hand and arm into the nonexistent fire. It required courage, almost more than he had. Yet he did it. For an instant he thought he felt heat, and then it was as he had expected it to be, and he almost laughed. There was no pain, no—

With a screech of agony and fury, the driver

29

yanked the seared flesh of his hand and wrist from the flames. Hastily he brushed the hot coals off, held his badly burned member close to his body, thought of the water in the tank down below, leaped to his feet to go immerse the seared wound in it, and—

He found himself sitting exactly as he had been sitting before, his hand and arm throbbing with pain. Meanwhile the old man sat across from him, the whole and perfect dipper in his hand, and the driver was certain that the old fool was laughing.

"All ... all right," the driver stammered through clenched teeth, "wh-what do you want of me? Money? Information? You can have it, anything you want. Just let me go."

"I can't," the old man replied, his voice filled with kindness and sorrow. "You have given me your shadow, and now it is time for you to learn."

"Learn? Learn what, and how?"

"In such a manner as this," the old man replied as he held the dipper over the fire once again. "Wind, fire, and water, the powers of mortality. Do you not wish to put your hand into the coolness of the water down in the tank? Arise, and behold."

The driver stared, rose slowly to his feet, and realized that he was indeed standing. He spun toward the tank of water that was below him, broke into a desperate sprint, and—

He found himself moving back up the hill away from the water, his face still turned toward the strange old man, a gust of wind whipping at him, and a cloud of steam rapidly dissipating into the darkness.

"No!" he screamed as he struggled with all his heart and will to go back down the hill. "Nooooo!"

Yet in spite of his efforts he was still climbing backward toward the darkened rock of the canyon rim, still moving away from the water in the tanks below, still facing the deep shadow of the old man.

"What do you want?" the driver screamed into the darkness at the face that he could not see. "What do you want? Why are you doing this to me? And how . . . *how* . . ."

"Why and how?" the old man responded as he sprinkled more water onto the hot coals. "I've told you, I want you to learn. You do not know yourself, and I am able to teach you of yourself because you have given me your shadow.

"But first your burn. It will stop hurting you now, but it will stay as you see it. I think," and now the old man paused, "I think you will have need of it again."

"What? Old man, you are the craziest . . ."

And then the driver began to learn.

31

The Challenge

The fire was lower, for much time had passed. The stars were brighter, the fitful wind seemed to have stopped, and out on the slick-rock a lone coyote yipped and cried out his loneliness for a companion but was not answered. Somewhere in the night a cricket chirped and was still, and the exhausted driver stared at the shadowy form before him.

It was hopeless, and now at last he knew that. Somehow the old man, whoever he was, had gained an incredible power over him, a power that made the driver, in spite of his own efforts and desires, no more than a puppet. Over and over he had tried to escape, over and over he had used the power of his mind or his words to try to intimidate the old man or to manipulate himself into freedom, and through it all the old man had simply sprinkled water and played with him as a cat might play with a mouse.

The driver thought for the thousandth time of his wife and family, and again he wondered how they would get along without him. For now he was afraid. More than ever before in his entire life he felt fear, and—

"Dear God," he cried out in his mind, "what is happening to me? Who is this old man, and how has he . . ."

"He is aware of you," the old man said.

"Wh-who?"

"God. He whom you were calling. That is why I have your shadow."

"I . . . I wish you would make some sense."

"Sense?" the old man repeated softly. "My dear friend, before your learning and your seeing are through, you will understand that my words make all the sense in the world."

"S-seeing?"

"Yes, you will see."

The driver stared into the fire, his mind whirling with questions that seemed to have no answers. "You talk about my shadow," he muttered, "but my shadow is . . . is not even tangible! How can you have it?"

"You still do not understand," the old man sighed, "and yet you should, for you have been given so much in the way of truth and light. Yet you have also turned away from it."

The driver stared, almost unable to believe, almost unable to comprehend the enormity of what he was hearing.

"T-turned away?" he cried indignantly. "How can you say that? I have turned away from nothing!"

"You have not? My son, are you as you once taught others to be?"

"What are you talking about?"

"Did you not once teach others the way of truth and light?"

"You mean my mission?"

"Yes, I mean when you last served God with your heart."

"You . . . you're crazy!"

"Am I?"

"You must be! That definitely was not the last time I served God! I have a testimony that the gospel is true. I am active in the Church, and I have been since I was a boy, my mission included! I know I am not perfect, but who is? Nevertheless, I have tried to keep the commandments. I have taught my children to believe and love the gospel, and my wife and I do our best to be of service to others. In other words, I have turned away from neither light nor truth!"

"Are you obedient in all things?"

"What?"

"Father gave the Evil One power to take light and truth from all who disobey His commandments. By choosing to be disobedient, my son, you have turned away from both light and truth, and so the Evil One has been given power over you."

"Old man," the driver fumed, "you have no right to insinuate such things!"

"I have every right in eternity," the old man stated quietly.

"Very well," the driver argued, his voice now firm in the righteousness of his position. "Show me why you have that right! If you have such power as you claim, show me!"

"He that seeketh for a sign—"

"Don't give me that, either! I'm not adulterous. But I am getting angry, and I demand proof from . . . no, I will be more polite than you have been. I am asking, and that is all."

"Ask," the old man then murmured, "and ye shall receive."

The driver grunted to show again his disgust. "One thing," he then added. "You show me, old man, and it is you who will receive, not me. You will receive proof that I am as I said. Besides, though this seems incredible to me, I think I know who you are, or at least who you represent. It seems to me that you are somehow connected to that Evil One you speak of, and I want you to know that I do not fear you. You have no power over me, none at all, for I rebuke you by the power and authority of the—"

Suddenly the old man held up his hand, and the driver found himself unable to go further.

"Behold," the old man said then, and with his hand he lifted the dipper and tipped it over the red coals of the dying fire.

36

The Seeings

"And the eyes of the blind," the old man said as the cloud of steam rose into the night wind, "shall see forth out of obscurity and out of darkness."

The driver stared, unable to move, unable to speak, and slowly he became aware that within the steam were faint images. At first he thought that he must be imagining those shapes, but quickly they took form. The swirling smoke became like the lighted backdrop of an enormous stage, and with a gasp of surprise the driver realized that he was seeing people against that backdrop, in scene after ever-changing scene.

More startled than he could imagine, the driver found himself looking around, though he had the feeling that such sensory perceptions as sight might have been unnecessary for what he was experiencing. Yet still he looked, and as he looked he understood that he was still aware of the fire and the sand and the old man who was yet seated before him.

No, at least those things had not changed.

Only . . . only somehow his vision was not confined by the narrow limitations of the darkness and the canyon. Somehow the steam and the smoke had created some sort of a huge, lighted, unlimited space in which he existed and upon which moved three-dimensional figures, speaking, breathing, living.

Squinting, the driver looked more closely at the figures and found that many of them seemed to be the same person. Even more closely he looked, and then, with sudden shocked understanding, he discovered that he was looking at himself.

"How . . . how . . . ?" he cried out into the limitless space within which he floated.

But for some reason his question could not be uttered. His tongue, no, his very being was bound. So the driver, transfixed, stared as he watched himself, somehow simultaneously (for there seemed to be no earlier and no later), in a wide variety of scenes.

He saw himself shielding his younger brother from an angry classmate when he had been in the third grade; he saw his newborn self being held aloft by a smiling doctor while his mother looked on in relief that she had delivered her baby safely; he saw himself getting his Eagle Scout award and graduating from seminary and high school; he saw himself as a two- or three-year-old sitting on his father's lap listening to his favorite story, and he determined that the girl leaning over him and listening too must be his older sister Janice, though of course he could not remember her at that age.

He saw himself in his seventh-grade science class trying over and over to get his project to work, and it was with startling clarity that he listened to the jeers of his classmates. More startling, however, were his own angry thoughts of revenge.

He saw his ninth-grade health class, heard Mr. Evans praising him for his ability to focus and concentrate on his text, when in reality he had been reading a novel in class. Then too he felt his own smugness that he should be so lauded in front of the others, and he heard clearly his thoughts of self-satisfied pride.

He saw himself standing helplessly while his father walked out of their home to begin what actually became a nasty divorce, and again he could hear his thoughts pleading with his father to stay, please to stay. He saw the tears that came then into his six-year-old eyes, and he saw his mother trying to comfort a hurt that he knew would not go away. Nor, he knew, would he let it. On this strange, other-worldly stage he could see clearly that he had clung to the hurt of his father's leaving in spite of his mother's efforts to comfort him because somehow he had felt that his hurt was all of his father that he had left to cling to.

All around him the driver saw scenes from his past, simple scenes, meaningless scenes, trivial incidents that he could not imagine meant anything at all. He saw himself riding a tricycle down a broken sidewalk; he saw himself climbing a tree; he saw himself falling down as he tried to jump rope with his older sister; he saw himself flying a kite with his younger brother and playing dolls with his sister and her friends; and he saw himself turning and walking nonchalantly away from a boy he recognized as his friend Mike, walking away even while Mike was pleading for him to stay and play.

As he gazed about, the driver noticed that he was seeing both happy moments and miserable moments, and with a shock he realized that much of the misery he had always blamed upon others had actually originated within himself. He saw with shame how he had turned away from the sincere desire for friendship offered by Big Jim, his mother's new husband, and he saw the very thought itself: "I'm

39

not going to love another dad, because he'll probably want to go away too." He saw himself watching
from the doorway as his mother came up the steps
with his new baby brother, saw and heard his mental
decision not to like the child no matter what happened, and yet saw too the moment he had saved his
baby brother's life by dislodging a bit of food he had
choked on.

There were other incidents—dates and parties
with girls, athletic meets, a day when he had sluffed
school with his buddies, and exams; and through it
all was his stiffnecked aloofness from his stepfather,
Big Jim, who had become, in his opinion, the family
clown because of his bumbling attempts to be liked.
There was also his careful selection of friends, chosen not because he liked or disliked them, but because they belonged to one group or another that
he wanted to be a part of.

Then too there were incidents from his life in
church—his baptism and his wish to go swimming
in the font, his ordination to the priesthood and his
calling as deacons quorum secretary. He saw himself blessing the sacrament and heard his profane
conversation with the other priests both before and
after the ordinance had been performed; he heard
too his terribly inappropriate thoughts as he sat at
the sacrament table and gazed down upon an im-
modestly dressed young woman whose name, even
now, he could not remember, but who had always
sat directly before and below his position at the
table.

He saw the string of five Sunday School teachers
he and his friends had driven from their classroom
the year he was fifteen, even heard himself instigat-
ing the others to ignore all questions from those
teachers or else turn the teachers' questions into
jokes.

Yet he also saw himself standing at a pulpit bear-

40

ing his testimony, and he saw the words coming from his mind as well as his mouth, words that declared truthfully that he *did* believe!

There was a gradual change then, and with relief the driver saw himself at age eighteen attempting to help his teachers with their lessons by being cooperative. He saw himself in a meeting listening and trying to understand the message of a speaker who he recalled had been a high councilor. He saw himself trying to get his younger brothers dressed and ready for church on time; he saw his mother hand him his mission call and could clearly hear his excitement as he read the call to Chicago, Illinois.

Then he was aware of scenes from his mission—tracting in Davenport, Iowa; teaching and bearing testimony and baptizing in Lombard and Elmhurst, Illinois; mornings in Pontiac when he could hear his thoughts declaring that he didn't care *what* the rules were, he was not getting up that early. Yet he also saw hours of diligent study and prayer while he labored in Rockford, Illinois, and Mt. Pleasant, Iowa; saw his spiritual side growing; saw himself showing young elders better ways to approach people and teach them the gospel; saw himself struggling with a companion in Rock Island and solving his problems with that poor conscience-stricken elder through fasting and mighty faith.

All of these things were there in the smoke and haze before the driver, all open, all honest, all exact pictures of events that he had seen or caused or heard or said or thought. In not one of them was there room for question or doubt; in not one of them did he feel praise or condemnation. They were simply there, for him to evaluate.

Yet as the smoke and the images at last began to fade, the driver found himself deeply relieved and just as deeply troubled.

"Old man," he asked when at last only the night

41

and the fire were left, "how on earth did you do that?"

"How is not important," the old man answered honestly.

"Not important? Old man, you don't realize what you have done. Why, if I could get that drug and market it to the right sources, you and I could *both* become mill—"

Once again the driver was unable to continue. His mouth was open, the word was created within his mind, and his tongue had formed the sounds of it, and yet he was frozen, unable to move, silent. He tried to say it once more but could not even move, let alone speak.

"Old man," his mind screamed, "why—"

"My son," the old man said softly, "I have told you there was no drug, and I do not lie. You saw what you saw because it is there. There is no 'how' to it. You saw it because you lived or thought or spoke it. That is all."

"All . . all right," the driver gasped, once again able to speak. "I . . . I will accept that, at least for now. But I do want an answer to this, and I would like to know now. Why have I seen this?"

"Why?"

"Yes. What is the point of showing me all those trivial events that I can't even remember?"

"My dear friend," the old man responded, "I showed you nothing. You saw your memories. And nothing you saw was trivial."

"Oh, come on! Tell me that riding my tricycle down a sidewalk was a significant event in my life."

The old man seemed, in the darkness of his face, to be smiling. "The things you saw," he said then, "are the things your own heart considered as significant. Each moment of your life has been recorded, and none of it is considered trivial to God because He gave each of those moments to you. They were each and every one an eternal building block in your life. You yourself chose the particular blocks or moments you wished to review."

"Well," the driver declared, leaning back on his elbow again, "I hate to say this, old man, but I'm a hard sale. I don't buy any of this. I still think some sort of drug is the answer, and I think that is probably why I recalled so much nonsense from my past. Now level with me. How soon will the drug wear off, and how can I get hold of a little of it?"

Slowly the old man shook his head, and the driver had the distinct impression that the hidden face was filled with sadness.

"As though in stone," the old man said softly.

"Pardon me?"

"Your ways. My son, why do you insist so forcefully that I take and keep your shadow?"

"Oh, come on," the driver growled, "let's not go through that nonsense again. I'm tired, and I don't feel like playing your game any longer. Just tell me how long this drug will last, and I'll hit the sack and sleep it off."

"How do you feel about what you saw in the smoke?" the old man asked, ignoring the driver's statement.

"What?"

"How did you feel as you watched those few portions of your life? Did you like yourself as you watched those events, or did you not?"

The driver stirred at the sand with his finger. He didn't want to answer, not at all. But for some reason he knew he would, and in his heart he clearly understood that there was nothing on earth he could do about it.

"Both, I suppose," he finally said, knowing that he had to play this silly game out to the end, even if he didn't understand why. "There was quite a bit that I liked, and quite a bit that I didn't."

"Is that all?"

"No, actually it isn't."

"Well?"

"I . . . uh . . . well, I guess I'm just thankful that I finally grew up."

"What do you mean?"

"I can't explain it. You'd have to have seen the same things that I saw."

"And you think I didn't?"

"Of course you didn't! I was the one you drugged."

"And so I did not see your father reading to you, or see him leaving home, or see your rejection of your mother or her new husband?"

The driver stared, his heart hammering within his chest. "How . . . how . . ."

"My dear friend, you have given me your shadow."

"But I don't . . ."

"In due time all these questions will be answered. Now tell me what you mean by feeling thankful that you grew up."

"Who . . . who *are* you?"

"What did you mean by your statement?"

The driver was suddenly angry. This was crazy, he was crazy, the old man was crazy! Why should he sit and answer all these foolish questions that had so little to do with anything? Why should he stay there at all? Just because his mind had been weakened by thirst and further twisted by the drug was no reason he had to put up with the degradation he was experiencing. The desert was all around him; it was a wide and empty country, and there was nothing that could prevent him from camping elsewhere.

Accordingly he rose abruptly to his feet, grimly smiled his triumph that the old man had not stopped him, turned toward the hill and his jeep, and—

"In answer to your question," the driver said quietly as he sat motionless before the glowing fire, unable to do anything at all but respond, "it took a while, but I finally got my act together."

"Your act? Is that what you saw in the smoke? An act?"

"Of course not," the driver growled. "That is only a figure of speech. What I meant was that I am glad I repented of the stupid things I did as a kid. I'm glad I finally got my priorities straight and became spiritually active in the Church. That's all I meant."

"Yes?"

"Yes what?"

"Is that good, being active in the Church?"

"Of course! Aren't you . . . I mean, well, I assumed you were a Mormon. Uh . . . do you believe in Jesus Christ?"

"I *live* for Christ."

"Well, so do I. That's why I am active in the Church, the Mormon Church, I mean. What about you? You talk like a Mormon. Aren't you involved in the Church?"

"I live the gospel."

"Those are synonymous terms, old man."

"Are they?"

"Yes, they are. By the way, the drug you gave me in that water, peyote or whatever it was? Actually, I'm glad you did it. Viewing my memories has given me a good feeling. If I can just keep going reasonably straight, if I can just keep active and willing to serve in the Church, then when I die I shouldn't have too much to worry about. I appreciate being able to see that."

The old man leaned forward. "You seem to be saying that you feel yourself to be a righteous man."

"Not *totally* righteous," the driver stated quickly, hoping that he had not given the old man the wrong impression. "No one is. Still, *if* you saw those hallucinations, then you also saw where my heart was in those scenes from my mission. Nothing has changed since then, either. I walk uprightly as well as I am able, and I repent quickly when I realize that I have done something wrong. I pay a full tithing plus all the little extras that the Church asks for; I go to the temple several times a year; I see to it that my kids go to all their meetings; I get my home teaching done almost every month; I never turn down a Church calling, and I support my wife in hers. I even went to youth conference three years ago and took a van full of noisy teenagers, and that ought to earn *any* man some blessings."

The driver smiled at his own little bit of humor, but he could not tell if the old man appreciated it or not. For a long time then it was quiet. The wind whispered past him and kicked a few sparks up into the darkness, and the driver wondered again what was happening to him. How had he fallen into this mess? What kind of drug could the old man have given him that would enable him to recall with such vividness all those old, forgotten memories?

Of course, he knew that the old man had not seen any of the things he himself had seen. Why, the idea was ludicrous. The sly old fool had known what the driver had seen while he was hallucinating simply because he had paid attention. No doubt the driver had been rambling. He had seen others do that, talk and talk while they were delirious. Drugged, he had obviously been delirious too, and no doubt his mouth had been running off the whole time.

Oh, if only he could find out what that drug had been. With the right approach, he could make a killing just selling it to medical facilities. On the other hand, he could keep the secret of the drug and learn all about it. Then he could take it, find a simple unobtrusive way to slip it to his clients, and, administered in the right quantities, it would set them up perfectly so that they would see, well, all their past accidents, for instance. Or their narrow escapes from death. Then wouldn't they plead for his insurance!

47

The driver stared into the fire, that amazing new idea filling his mind. He became more excited by the moment because of the incredible potential of it. Medical facilities? He would *never* market that drug. It would be his own personal Ark of the Covenant. Like the Israelites who carried their ancient ark into battle, he would take his drug into a client's home and would never fail!

Imagine, a 100-percent success ratio! Why, his position as a regional representative would be only temporary. In just months, maybe even weeks, he would be in a vice-president's office. After that would come president, and then, who could tell. Chairman of the board, probably, and then on and on.

Incredible. And all because he had stumbled onto this crazy old man. See, he would tell his wife, he truly *was* being blessed. Now all he had to do—

"Old man," he said, using his friendliest voice, "I'd like to help you out. I really would. How would you like a new home, say, with a swimming pool and air conditioning?"

"I have no need."

"No need? But . . . but . . . No, of course you

don't. But I'll tell you what. I've never known one of your people yet who didn't love horses. How would you like a thoroughbred stallion—a stallion and, say, a dozen mares?"

The old man sat silently, and the driver's heart was filled with sudden hope. He was going to do it! He was—

"I'll tell you what," he said. "I'll throw in a corral with the horses. I'll even build a barn, and—"

"My friend, of what good is a horse, or even a hundred horses, to the Taker of Shadows?"

Startled, the driver mentally sat back, his mind scrambling frantically for another direction. "No," he said quickly while his mind groped forward, "I should have known that. You are above such things, and I was blind to have missed it. No, your concerns are for . . . for your *people*, and that is commendable. I respect you for that, very much. In fact, I would like to offer my services to your people too. I would like to set up a scholarship fund, maybe two. Then I should like to establish, in due time, of course, a cultural center where your people can develop their arts and crafts, their native talents. Why, with our earnings from that dru . . . er, my insurance business—"

"Are you an honest man?"

"What?"

The old man leaned forward. "I asked if you were honest in your dealings with others."

"Hey," the driver said, smiling amiably and completely comfortable with the question. "What is this, a temple recommend interview? I told you, I'm active in the Church. I hold a temple recommend; to get that I must answer a similar question, and my answer has always been yes. It still is. Besides, I've always done everything I could to see that the needs of others were taken care of, and as you know, that is a higher level of honesty than even most Mormons live. Why, when you and I become partners . . ."

"My son?"

"Yes?"

"Would you tell me about yourself and Homer Bean?"

49

The Journey

Homer Bean.

His heart suddenly pounding with nameless fear, the driver stared into the blackness that sat across the fire from him. How had the old man known of Homer? How on earth—

Quickly he reached out, took up a stick, and worked it into the hot coals. As the flames licked up he added another stick and then another, until shortly there was a well-established fire. In the light, then, he gazed at the old man, doing his best to see into the darkness under his strange hat.

But no, even in the light he could not see! All he could see was shadow . . . nothing but shadow! But that made no sense at all. The light of the fire was bright, it was below the brim of the old man's hat, and yet still his face was hidden. How could that be?

"I have told you, my son."

"You . . . you have told me what?"

"That you have given me your shadow. From this time forward your vision of things eternal will be obscured. Now, will you please tell me of Homer Bean."

"Did I do a little rambling about him too?" the

driver asked, almost relieved that he could avoid discussing that nightmare topic of shadows.

"Yes, the things of your heart have been expressed. Thus I know somewhat of how you feel about him."

"Ignore all that nonsense, old man. You can't pay attention to the demented ramblings of a drugged man. Besides, Homer and I go back a long way. We work for the same company, and I think a lot of him."

"Only he is, as you said, a loser."

"Did I say that?"

The old man motioned yes with his hand, and the driver dropped his head. "He and I do go about things a little differently," he said quietly, "but that doesn't mean that Homer is a loser. In fact, he is a great man, always has been, and I would do anything for him. If I said he is a loser, forget it. He'll go a long way, and I intend to do everything in my power to help him."

"You have authority over him?"

The driver nodded.

"Why would you do that? Help him, I mean."

"I told you. Homer and I have been close friends for over fifteen years. I guess you could say I owe him too, and he whom I owe, I pay. That's part of my personal creed, part of the honesty you asked about earlier."

"Ah," the old man said, speaking more to himself than he was to the driver. "It seems to me, then, that it is time."

"Time for what?"

"Time for the beginnings of your seeing and thus your learning." With an easy movement the old man lifted the dipper and poured some of its contents onto the fire.

There was an instant hiss as smoke and steam

billowed upward. A mighty wind came from nowhere and tugged at the driver, and for a heartbeat he thought he would literally be lifted from the earth and carried away with the smoke. But then the wind abated, the smoke began to clear, and—

Figures!

Again the driver could see figures, but this time they were not as before. The narrow defile in the slick-rock was gone, and the fire and the old man were gone too. Now he was somewhere else, in a place he had never before been. It was a wide land, and flat. Distant hills rose beyond him, but here only small gullies cut the surface of the earth, small gullies and occasional humps that might be called hills.

No, the driver was certain that he had never seen this place before. Nor had he ever seen these people.They were seated and standing in groups, talking or being silent, cooking or eating or just relaxing, and none of them looked familiar at all. Nor could he hear any sound but the ever-present wind. He was just there, seeing but unseen, observing but able to hear nothing but the comments of the old man.

He studied the people who were all about him, and he noticed finally that the weather had changed. There were patches of snow on the ground, the people were bundled up, and—

And then the driver noticed that in spite of the cold there were children playing. Then he saw that it was near dark and that fires dotted the ground between the wagons, fires over which many of the women were cooking—

Wagons? Women cooking over open fires?

"Old man," he whispered fearfully, "where—"

"Today and in times past you have wondered concerning these people," the old man answered easily from behind him. "Because of that, it has been determined that you may see them. They have camped here at Forty Mile Camp, preparing for what will become, for them, the greatest journey of their lives, their descent through Hole-in-the-Rock and their trek through the country beyond."

"This . . . this is *them?*" the driver asked incredulously. "You . . . you've got to be kidding!"

"I am not. You are seeing them as they were, or are, if you prefer."

"But . . . but how . . ."

"All the deeds of man are recorded," the old man answered. "But of course you know that, for you have taught it."

"That's true," the driver whispered, "only I didn't know—"

"That such deeds could be seen again?" the old man continued for him. "Of course they can. Of what use would a record be if it could not be read? Or seen? Or experienced, if need be?"

"And these people are the actual Hole-in-the-Rock pioneers?"

"Some call them pioneers," the old man answered obliquely, "but they do not think so of themselves. They think of themselves as missionaries, missionaries to the Lamanites. You, my friend, have also called them foolish, or, even worse, insane."

"Well, they were!" the driver protested. "I've been over their trail, and all they would have had to do was go north by Green River or south into Arizona and they would have avoided this desolate stretch of real estate."

"Yes, of course you are right, at least as far as the understanding of man is concerned."

"What do you mean?"

"Do you see that man in the black coat?"

"The one standing off alone?"

"Yes. His name is Silas S. Smith. He has been called by John Taylor, the Church's new president, to preside over these people."

"So he's the one who was . . . is responsible for the horror they all went through?"

"Perhaps that is so. He is surely carrying the emotional burden of it. However, Charles Hall over there at the farthest fire gave the scouting report suggesting that the route was passable. Based upon that report they all voted to take the shortcut and gathered at this place. They learned from their scouts only yesterday what was actually ahead of them. Now they see the mistake of their decision, but still they are stuck."

"Charles Hall? Why did he make a dumb report like that?"

"His wife was expecting a baby, and he was worried about her. He simply did not feel he had time to cover all that wilderness and still be home with her."

"Well, whatever his report was like, now they know. And here is where they did the stupidest thing of all."

"Why is that, my son?"

"Why? Old man, right here they could have turned around and gone back. Anyone with any sense at all—"

"They cannot go back. The snow in the pass is already too deep for so many to pass through it."

"Well then, they could have waited right here until spring. Surely it would have been no more difficult than—"

"They have been called by a prophet of God to go to Montezuma Creek. He did not call them to go next year, nor did he call them to go last year. He called them to go *now*."

"Well, I *still* think what they did was stupid. I don't think the Lord would have minded—"

"Could the Lord have made the snow in the mountains fall less deeply?" the old man asked.

"Yes, but—"

"But He didn't. Could He have inspired President Taylor to send them a message telling them to wait?"

"Well, sure. The Lord can do anything He wants. Still—"

"Still none of those things has happened," the old man interrupted quietly. "The Lord recognizes that men are strengthened by overcoming trials and obstacles and gives us the strength to endure them. Of course it will be difficult for these people, but the journey will also be a great builder of their faith, and their dedication to the Lord will increase a hundredfold. Thus in the long run it will turn out to be a wonderful blessing for every one of them."

The driver stared around him at the large scattered group of huddled figures. "I don't know," he finally responded. "I still think—"

"Actually," the old man interrupted again, "that is why they are called Saints. No matter how difficult things have become, no matter whose fault any of this is, they are willing to be obedient to the Lord and His earthly representative. Thus it will be that here almost all of them will begin a journey that will determine a righteous course not only for their own lives, but for the lives of multitudes of their descendants who will also choose obedience, because of their ancestors, through many generations yet to come.

"And that, my son, is why we are here. As you see them, so too will you see your own beginnings."

"My birth? I already—"

"No," the old man softly interrupted, "that was an entry more than a beginning. A life truly begins when one consciously chooses the course of his future. Your beginning is now before you, a beginning that could, if it were allowed to continue, determine, for generations of Father's children, the course of their eternities."

"What?" the driver questioned. "But you don't . . . you can't . . . I feel like I am going crazy. Why can't you tell me what is going on?"

"Knock," the old man interrupted softly, "and it shall be opened unto you."

And then, as the driver stared, the figures grew faint in the mist. The wind howled, and he felt again that impossibly helpless feeling that he was adrift somewhere in the immensity of space.

He tried to cry out but couldn't; he tried to find something solid to cling to, but couldn't; he was filled with unspeakable terror that he was in this place of emptiness and could do nothing about it.

Then around him light began to grow, and instantly he was aware of another figure, one growing rapidly more distinct. Only this one was no pioneer, for he was pedaling a bicycle down a busy street.

The driver stared. There was something about that man and that particular street, something familiar, something—

"Hey there! Watch out!"

The man on the bicycle, hurrying home from his classes at BYU, glanced toward the sound of the voice and saw a young man on the nearby sidewalk staring at him and past him.

No one he knew, he thought instantly. Probably just—
"Hey! Look out!"

The man turned his head, saw too late the gaping construction ditch in the road before him, and with a sinking sensation knew that he could never stop in time. Still, he grabbed both handbrakes, started to slide, and felt a sudden impact, and the next thing he knew he was rolling across a lawn, all tangled up with another human being.

When he finally stopped rolling and got his bearings, he was surprised to find himself lying on the grass beside the young man who had been on the sidewalk yelling at him.

"Hi," the fellow said, smiling widely as he dusted himself off and sat up. "Sorry about dumping you like that. My name's Bean, Homer Bean."

"You mean like string bean?"

"No," Homer Bean laughed. "With a body like mine, I'd say lima bean."

Both young men laughed, and Homer Bean leaped to his feet and helped the other up.

"I hope your bike's okay," he said sincerely. "I think it went into the hole."

Together they walked over and looked, and indeed that was where the bicycle had gone. It was ten feet down, lying on its side, and looked pretty well battered up.

"Wow," the rider said, "I'm glad I didn't go down there with it. Hey, man, you saved my life!"

Homer Bean shook his head vigorously. "Not me. I was just lucky enough to be here. Say, aren't you in old Benson's business class?"

"Yeah. Why?"

"I'm in there too. He's a great teacher, don't you think?"

"If you want to know the truth, I think he's a pain in the neck."

They both laughed, and Homer Bean scrambled down into the trench. Grabbing the bike he hefted it up to the rider, who hauled the damaged machine out of the hole. Then Homer climbed out, and together they walked toward the rider's small apartment.

58

"*You going into business?*" *Homer Bean asked.*

"*I hope to. How about yourself?*"

"*I don't know. I've been planning on it, but now I'm not sure.*"

"*What's the problem?*"

"*Well, I've been watching business people lately, and I don't know if I can hack their lifestyle.*"

"*You mean the money?*"

"*No,*" *Homer Bean answered thoughtfully.* "*I don't know how to explain this, but I don't* think *like most business people do. I'm not even sure I want to.*"

"*I . . . I guess I don't understand. I love how business people think; the decision making, the jockeying for position and power, the manipulating of ways and means so that wealth comes toward you rather than away from you. To me, that is the height of excitement, and I can't imagine that someone else might feel differently.*"

"*Some do,*" *Homer Bean declared,* "*but it goes deeper than that. For instance, I can't seem to get excited about accumulating either wealth or power. Of course I need a little, more or less, of each. But to accumulate either one just for the sake of getting them, well, I'm not very interested. Anyway, lately I think I've begun to understand why.*"

"*And?*"

"*Well, I think it is something that we brought with us from before our births, like a gift or talent. You know how the scripture says that some will become priests and kings? The way I look at it, in premortal life we tended to gravitate toward, and focus on, one or the other of those two positions.*"

"*What?*"

"*Strange idea, isn't it. Of course, it's not Church doctrine, but the more I think about it, the more sense it makes, at least for me.*"

"*Can you explain it?*"

"*Sure, I guess so. If in the spirit world a man focused on priestly duties, his growth was in things spiritual, and he brought those attitudes and abilities with him to mortality. If, on the other hand, he focused on things kingly, then his growth was in things temporal, such as decision making. He also brought those attributes with him to mortality. As I see it, we are here now to round out our learning. I think in the premortal existence I leaned toward things priestly, and so now I am studying business, trying to become a whole eternal being. It's just that I don't . . . well, I don't like it very much."*

"I have never heard that thought," the rider declared. "If it is true, I wonder which I focused on."

"Are you kidding? Hey, I've watched you in class. You eat those simulated business situations up! I hate pressure like that, but you? You're a natural!"

"So you think I focused on kingly things?" the rider asked.

"I don't know that, of course, but from what I've seen, I'd say yes. Just think about how you make decisions. I've watched you, and you're like a shark going after dinner. Snap, snap, snap! You could easily be a king! Me, I agonize over every little thing, worrying about ramifications, wondering if someone will be hurt by what I decide or if someone else will be benefited more than another, and so on. I'd probably be the worst king in the world."

"Kings and priests, huh? What an interesting idea!"

"Well, it's something to think about."

For a moment the two walked in silence, and the rider did think. Was it possible? Could it be true that he had been prepared for eternities to become a successful businessman? In a way it made sense, for it was awfully easy for him to go snap, snap, snap. Of course, according to Homer, that meant that he was now to round things out, focus on things spiritual. But there was time for that after he had made it big, wasn't there? There had to be. After all, why waste talent? Didn't the Lord himself tell people not to hide their talents under a basket?

"I think you're right," he finally declared. "I do make

*decisions fast, and I always do best under pressure. When
we had those baptism contests on my mission, I always
won."*

"Where did you go?"

"Chicago."

*"No kidding? Northern States, isn't it? I was in the
East Central States."*

*"Is that right? Hey, man, I heard that's where the pres-
sure was really on!"*

*"I'll say it was," Homer Bean agreed. "That's why I
don't like pressure now, I think. I usually baptized, but I
tried to make sure they were converts rather than num-
bers."*

"Well, when I was assistant—"

"You called them that?"

*"No, we called ourselves counselors, but now it's
changed, so I just say assistant. Anyway, it seems to me,
and it did then, that once a person is baptized, no matter
how you get them in the water, they get the Holy Ghost, and
then with the Lord's help they can be on their way. That's
why we pushed our elders into baptizing."*

*"Yeah," Homer Bean agreed, "some elders had that
philosophy in my mission too. I just didn't feel right about
it. I used to say, let the Holy Ghost do His work while I
teach and bear testimony, give the folks challenges to pre-
pare for baptism by such-and-such a day, and work with
them toward that goal, but let* them *make the final decision. No phoney tricks or pressure sessions or any of that
stuff. I say, let the Lord put on the pressure, not the elders."*

"Were you ever an assistant?"

"I'll say not. I think I was the mission rebel."

*"You'd think differently if you had been in charge of
all the missionaries, and if every week you had had to answer to the mission president."*

*"Maybe, maybe not. Frankly, I doubt it. I never was a
very good yes man, and that's what some of the elders
seemed to be. It was like they didn't dare think for them-*

61

selves. By the way, what are you going to do about your bike?"

"Oh, I'll figure out something. Jeannie will get her check—"

"Is that your wife?"

"Yeah, three months now. Boy, is she something!"

Homer Bean nodded. "I'll bet she is. I got married last week, and my wife is pretty special too."

"What's her name?"

"Ann."

"That's great," the rider declared. "You know what? The four of us ought to get together and do something."

"Yeah, we should! I—uh-oh, I just thought of something. With your wife working, I'll bet you don't have very much time alone together."

"Sure we do. We're broke, but we'll do something cheap, roast hot dogs or something. You know, Homer Bean, I remember you now. You're the only one in class who aced that last exam."

Homer Bean dropped his head. "Yeah, I guess I got lucky on that one, all right."

"Luck, my eye. I heard some of the others talking. They said you'd aced every exam this year."

"Not true. I missed one."

"One what? You blew an exam?"

"No, I missed one question," Homer Bean mumbled. "I should have known it, too. I just—"

"Say, Homer," the rider said thoughtfully, "maybe we could get together and study, help each other out a little."

"Sure," Homer Bean agreed quickly. "That is, if it won't interfere with you and Jeannie."

"It won't interfere. Can you come?"

"You bet! In fact, if you want, we'll come over tonight."

"Great. Bring your wife, and we'll have those hot dogs too."

"Okay. Seven?"

"Great. And Homer, thanks for saving my bacon! That trench was deep!"
Homer waved his hand as if it were nothing, turned, and—

———————

"Can . . . can *you* see all that?" the driver asked as he stood on the sidewalk watching the two young men separate.

"Of course," the old man replied.

"Do you see . . . even the thoughts?"

"You mean your desire to use Homer Bean to get better grades even though you have nothing to give him in return?"

"It *is* me we're looking at, isn't it?" the driver asked, his mind still filled with hesitation. "I mean, I remember that trench. I have no doubt that Homer saved me from at least a serious injury. Now that I see it again, it looks likely that I might have been killed."

"You might have been."

"But how? Old man, what kind of a drug . . ."

"My son, the only drug has been your attitudes and actions, which have drugged you until you are beyond feeling. Besides, you ask how, but is how as important as why?"

"What do you mean?"

"Homer just saved your life. Don't you wonder that your motives could so quickly become selfish? Don't you wonder why that is so?"

"Hey, it wasn't really like that, and I'm not a selfish man! Sure those thoughts were there at first, but Homer and I became best friends, and if he helped me with my grades, I helped him with his marriage and other things even more. I mean, Ann was such a mousy little thing, and so Jeannie and I decided to spruce her up. We did, too. Jeannie taught her about makeup and clothes, and every time we got together I gave both of them a course in PMA, Positive Mental Attitude. I felt like I was back leading a couple of the slower elders and sisters in my mission.

"I helped Homer, too, when Ann wasn't around. Did you see how *he* was dressed in that vision or hallucination or whatever you call it? I don't know how he ever made it through a mission, but I don't wonder that he was never a leader! Talk about being a loser—"

"As though in stone," the old man declared sadly, and suddenly the driver was away again, drifting, and images were appearing, growing more vivid—

"So, Brother Franklin," the young missionary said sincerely, "your daughters have asked to be baptized, and we have come to get your permission."

The room where the three sat and stood was small and close, yet even there the tension was a huge and living thing. The two elders stood together facing the seated man, a giant who made no effort to hide his hatred.

"I ain't y'uns brother," the man growled angrily, "and y'uns didn't tell me y'uns names, neither."

"Elder Bean, and this is my companion, Elder Compton. Now about that permission, if you'd please sign . . ."

"Why, y'uns both no good scallywags, and I'm of a mind to beat both of y'uns to a bloody pulp!"

"I don't think you'd do that," Elder Bean declared quietly. "You see, we represent the Lord here in Tennessee, and—"

"The Lord! I don't want nothing to do with y'uns Mormon Lord! Now, y'uns have talked long enough. Hit the road!"

"No, Mr. Franklin, we won't go. Not until you have signed for your daughters. You see, they are fine girls. They will be a great strength to the branch here, and they have a great desire to do what is right—"

With a howl of rage the burly man rose to his feet, picked up his chair, and, swinging it above his head, he strode toward the two young missionaries. Elder Compton involuntarily stepped back, but Elder Bean moved not at all. His face was composed, and he stood still while the big man with the chair moved toward him, cursing.

"Mr. Franklin," the elder said firmly, "we have come to get permission for your daughters to be baptized, and we won't leave until . . ."

"A loser, my son?" the old man questioned. "Not a leader?"

"I . . . I must know how you do that!" the driver whispered. "If I had that secret—"

"Once again, how is not so important as why."

"Why?"

"Yes! Why do you judge such a man as a follower and a loser?"

"Because I know him! Besides, he told me that himself! He wasn't a zone leader, let alone a district leader. Any missionary worth anything at all is at least a district leader."

"And to you that is what being a leader means? Holding a position? Behold, and you shall see a true leader in the work of the Lord!"

The driver then watched with reluctant fascination as a young Elder Bean, with a brand-new companion beside him, defended the gospel of Jesus Christ for over three hours in a Tennessee cottage meeting where forty people and three ministers worked steadily to tear down the beliefs of the two of them. He saw the young missionaries stand forth in mighty testimony before two apostates. He saw them driven out of a home late one January night, struggle with their car, run out of gas twice, and at last get home with the help of a Brother Louis Beatty, and then he saw Elder Bean drop immediately to his knees to begin pleading with the Lord that he be allowed to go back to that home and bear his testimony one more time. He saw—

"My son," the old man declared as the images faded, "I would say that Elder Bean was one of the great warrior missionaries of this dispensation. Is that not a leader?"

"Well, maybe he was, and maybe he wasn't," the driver mumbled reluctantly. "The way I remember it, we *all* had tough missions."

"Yes," the old man agreed, "and many of you make your missions in mortality more difficult than they need be as well."

"Now wait a minute—"

"You were speaking of how you helped Homer Bean."

"Yes, I was. But more importantly, I want to know how you—"

"Homer Bean, my son."

The driver dropped his head, fighting with all his heart to keep from responding to the old man.

"As I said," he replied, "whether Homer was a good missionary or not, I was the one who taught him about clothing, colors, styles. I even worked on his language. He talked as if he were from Sanpete County, if you can believe it! And that was even after his mission! I'm telling you, old man, that initial selfish thought of mine sure didn't turn out to be a selfish deal. I gave Homer a lot more than he ever gave me."

"I'm sure you did," the old man agreed, "including the blame for getting the answers to that final exam you cheated on that year."

The driver stared. This wasn't possible! How could this senile old fool of an Indian know about such things as that? How could—

And then it hit him; suddenly he knew.

Homer Bean! Homer was behind all this! In his bitterness at not getting the regional representative position, he had concocted this crazy scheme. He had hired the old Indian with his potent drug, had given him all sorts of screwy information, had obtained the driver's destination from Jeannie, and—

"When did you meet Homer?" the driver asked quickly and offhandedly.

"I have not had that pleasure. My errand is otherwise."

"Come on, old man, I know a scam when I see one! And this is a setup, a scam. Poor old bitter Homer Bean put you up to this, and I know it. I'll tell you something, too. I apologized to Homer about that test. I explained how he could stand the hit but that it would kill me, and he agreed, so even if it was wrong, and I admit freely that it was, I repented!"

"Are you certain of that?"

"Am I certain? Of course I am! I just told you that I talked with Homer about it. What more—"

"Did you tell your professor? Did you inform the school that your grade was unjustified? Did you kneel before the Lord to seek forgiveness?"

The driver stared. Of course he hadn't done those things. He'd probably prayed about it, though he couldn't remember with certainty any such prayer. As far as the other things, however, he had most certainly not done them. That would have been scholastic suicide, for at the time he had not decided to leave school. Still, he *had* apologized to Homer, and so—

"Old man," the driver growled, "as I said, that exam is a dead issue. But I'll tell you something else that *isn't* a dead issue.

"Homer has *always* been jealous of me. I'm successful, my wife is beautiful, my children are outgoing and talented, and the list goes on. Meanwhile, in spite of what Jeannie and I tried to teach him, that poor guy's life is just the opposite from ours. Not a day goes by but he sits and eats his heart out—"

The driver was interrupted by a groan from the old man; the mist was there again, and in it the driver found himself staring at himself and Homer Bean. He watched as Homer spent a week helping him paint his house; he watched as Homer and Ann paid for a night out when both he and Jeannie were broke; he watched as Homer and Ann knelt in the privacy of their bedroom and prayed that he and Jeannie would be empowered to earn the money they so badly needed for tuition; he watched as Homer delivered a sack of groceries to the driver's small home; he watched as Homer and Ann laughed happily as they fixed up a small room in their own tiny old home; he watched as they laughed at the antics of their first little child; he watched as Homer prayed again that the driver would be forgiven for cheating on the final exam—

"My son, are those the actions of a jealous man?"

"You don't understand!" the driver shouted. "Those are incidents, selected incidents, and they don't represent the true picture. I have always had Homer's best interests at heart. Besides, I already told you that I apologized for cheating. I repented, and so it is gone, wiped away. Anyway, with his good

grades Homer could take the heat for that and survive. If I had stayed in school, it would have ruined
me. Why, I even got him his job to show him how
sorry I was! And it's a good thing I did. He'd probably still be looking for work if I hadn't got him
started.

"I'll tell you something else. With his brown,
curled-up shoes and his baggy pants, he didn't look
like much; never has and probably never will. But I
told the man who was hiring about Homer's grades
and his fine mind and that we went way back together, and so Homer got hired. Don't you see? I
got Homer his job! Now don't you tell me I haven't
been thinking of him!"

Instead of answering, the old man lifted the dipper he still held in his hand, tipped it, and—

"Wh-where are we?" the driver whispered scant
seconds later. "And what are they *doing?*"

"They're getting ready to go down that crevice
in the cliff."

"You're kidding!"

"I'm not, and neither are they. That road is what
they called the Hole-in-the-Rock."

"That's *it?* I mean, I'd heard—"

"Steep, isn't it. Platte D. Lyman, who is their new
leader, used a square and a level and has determined that the grade is almost 50 percent."

"But . . . how can *anything* go down something
that steep?"

"It is a dangerous trail, that is certain. Do you see
that team of horses? They're blind and will go
where Brother Barton leads them. They don't know
that road is so steep, and so they will go down it
rather easily. Watch."

"But he doesn't have any help!"

"True, but it is sundown, and he has decided that he cannot wait for the ten men and their rope to help hold him back."

"He's crazy! No one can do that alone."

"He has rough-locked his wheels and expects that that will be enough. There he goes!"

The driver stared as the small, wiry man urged his team and wagon over the edge and down onto the incredibly precipitous roadway that had been blasted out of the cliff. He saw the horses buck-jumping downward while the wagon slid behind them, saw everything, wagon and horses together, begin sliding, and thirty seconds later saw the whole group come to an upright stop at the first station, three hundred feet below.

"What happened?" the driver asked quickly.

"His rough-lock broke, but the Lord was watching and allowed the broken chain to flip a lap around the felloe in such a manner that it locked it again. Thus Joseph Barton has been saved to bring up a righteous posterity."

Amazed, the driver turned once again to gaze at the road down through the Hole. Actually, however, it was not a road at all, but merely a slit in the cliff that dropped for two thousand feet in a quarter of a mile of horizontal distance, going almost straight down. Yet in this one spot these people had chiseled a cut for one wheel and then drilled holes for poles that had then been inserted and covered with brush and dirt as a tacked-on roadway for the other wheel. On that ridiculous pathway and nothing else they were trusting their lives and possessions, intent only on getting to the bottom.

"They're crazy," the driver muttered as he shook his head. "Nothing can stay on a road like that!"

70

"That is called Uncle Ben's Dugway, named in honor of its engineer, Benjamin Perkins. It was one of the most difficult portions of the Hole."

"I still say they are crazy!"

"Dedicated," the old man replied. "Nothing can dissuade them in their descent. Like you, my son. Dedicated in your efforts to reach the depths of hell, no matter who tries to help you climb to loftier heights."

The driver spun around. "What sort of a crack is that?"

"A sincere one."

"I don't like the tone of your voice, old man. Neither do I like your filthy accusations!"

The old man stood then, completely still, while all around him and the driver, people and horses and cattle and dogs scurried about, lining up for the crossing of the Colorado River that wound past the bottom of the Hole.

"My son," the old man declared softly, "they had to descend only two thousand feet. Your descent is eternal, because you made the decision to go downward and then set your decision as if in stone. You were given the choice and you took it, and now I have your shadow."

Raising his arm then, the old man gazed sternly at the driver. "Behold!" he declared. "You shall now begin to see."

"Homer," the salesman declared, "I'm so angry I feel like swearing. You'd think they'd have seen it."

"They should have, all right."

"I'll say they should have, the jerks!"

"Well, it wasn't the company's fault."

"Maybe, but they still should have seen it. Hancock.

That dirty, rotten crook! You'd think the man upstairs could see through him. I'd earned that five-hundred-dollar bonus, not him. He cheated me out of it! He really did!"

Homer Bean reached out and placed his hand on his friend's arm. "I know he did. In fact, everybody in the office knows you'd been cultivating Scrunch for weeks, setting them up for a group policy."

"Yeah. Scrunch Clamping Products. My customer, and the way for that bum Hancock to get my bonus."

"You could go to the boss about it."

The salesman looked at Homer Bean in disgust. "Oh sure, and get the reputation of being a poor loser? No thanks, brother. I'd rather fight fire with fire."

"What do you mean?"

"Just what I said. He took my client, I'll get a few of his. Hancock stole my bonus, but before I'm through he'll lose multiples of that five hundred dollars. In fact, before I'm through, he'll be gone, clear out of the business!"

Homer Bean stared at the floor, his expression pained and nervous. He crossed his legs, uncrossed them, crossed them again, cleared his throat, and finally spoke. "Uh . . . I know you need the money, but doesn't that make you the same as Hancock?"

The salesman snorted. "I'll say not! That skunk is as dishonest as they come! I'm only paying him back!"

"I don't mean to get preachy, but what about turning the other cheek, praying for them which despitefully use you, and leaving revenge to the Lord?"

"Homer, you have a lot to learn about business, I'll tell you that. In church you use that turn-the-other-cheek stuff, and probably during the millennium. But right now, out here in the real world, it is do unto others before they can do unto you. It's the law of the jungle! Hancock will cheat me again and you know it, so I'll get him before he has the chance. Besides, a dirty crook like Hancock doesn't deserve to be a salesman for AMPAX."

"But . . . but how? How will you do it?"

The salesman grinned. "I know his secretary," he said. "She likes me, and if I ask her right, I'll end up with a list of every client old Hancock ever had."

Homer Bean stared at the floor for a moment before speaking. "I . . . I don't know," he said quietly. "I really think you ought to let the boss or one of his superiors take care of it."

"Homer, I don't understand how a man as smart as you are can be so dumb. I don't squeal on Hancock, I don't create waves, and while he is going under I'll just keep looking better and making more money. It's the perfect setup."

73

Homer Bean shook his head. "No, no it isn't!" he finally declared. "What you will be doing is flat-out dishonest and wrong. I know it, and deep down, so do you."

"What I know is that I need to survive so that Jeannie and I can pay our bills. We made those obligations, we needed that five hundred bucks and had even prayed that we could get it so we could pay our creditors, and if we don't pay, that's dishonest! Until Hancock stole it, we were even going to pay our tithing out of that bonus.

"As far as right or wrong goes, Homer, this isn't the mission field. This is the real world, where a man survives by eliminating the competition. And a good businessman does that in any way he can. I'll tell you what, old friend, today the decision has been made. I'm going to survive!*"*

"Well, I still don't think you'd better do it."

"Hey, my friend, it's my life, and don't you forget it!"

His head down with discouragement, Homer Bean turned sadly away—

"Were you warned?" the old man asked quietly.

"Warned?" the driver snarled. "I didn't need any warning! Besides, who is Homer Bean anyway, and what does he know about business? For that matter, what do *you* know about business, living out here in the sticks? I'm telling you, in that cutthroat world where I live, things aren't black and white, right and wrong. They are gray. In fact, they are thousands of shades of gray. A man simply does what he must do in order to survive."

"And you feel good about that? About yourself?"

"Feel good? Of course I do! My family lives well, my kids get the best teachers and opportunities, and I pay a whole lot of tithing. Besides that, my time has become more free, so I have been able to do a better job in my church work. In one way or another I have helped out every elder in my quorum. Shouldn't I feel good?"

The old man did not answer but lifted the dipper and—

"Hey," the driver cried, looking around, "it's snowing!"

"It does that a lot during these high desert winters. As you might notice, these folks are still traveling. You might note also that it doesn't seem to slow them down."

"Not so a man would notice," the driver said as he looked around at the heavily clothed people. He and the old man stood in a cut in the rock that led upward, a cut that had been a natural ravine. Now, however, the cut was filled with people, men and boys and even women. All were busy building up what the driver assumed would be a road grade. In places the rock had been hammered and blasted out; in others, where the slope fell too steeply away, the rocks had been stacked up and filled behind with dirt, making an almost level track.

"Is this Cottonwood? Isn't this where I was earlier?"

"Yes. You spilled your water up there, just about a mile from where they will establish what they will call their Cheese Camp. Below and behind us is Cottonwood Wash, the terrible Sand Hill, and Register Rocks. This hole they are working in is called the Dugway."

"I've always thought it was too narrow for wagons to get through," the driver said as he examined the new road.

"Actually it isn't," the old man responded. "You see, the Saints' wagons aren't very large. The wagon boxes are only three feet by seven feet by a foot deep, and the wheels are just four feet apart. They don't need a lot of room."

75

"You mean these people carried everything they owned in . . . in . . ."

"Yes, they did. And they were comfortable, too, at least by their standards."

The driver shook his head in amazement, and again he watched in silence. Here and there people huddled around fires; two blacksmiths worked steadily at their forges; and all around the camp, scattered livestock pawed at the snow trying to find forage. Above them, up the draw a few hundred yards, several men and horses waited. At last the signal was given. The horses were led down through the cut and harnessed to strings of singletrees and doubletrees, which were hooked to the tongue of the first wagon by two men who lay in the snow to do it, and with the cracking of several whips the animals began dragging the heavy wagon upward.

On that first wagon were seven span of horses, and when some of them fell to their knees and were fighting to get a foothold, the still-erect horses were plunging upward against the horrid grade. Here and there men were beating the animals continuously so that they would keep pulling; some of the horses were in spasms and near convulsions from exhaustion, and where the wagon and teams had passed, the way was covered with blood and matted hair from the forelegs of the struggling animals.

Nor did the horses work alone. Men with ropes staggered through the snow, pulling with all their hearts to help the horses along. It was hard work every inch of the way, but when one man dropped out from exhaustion, another would take his place. Thus the wagon, being pulled by those several span of horses and pulled and pushed by dozens of men and women, slowly moved upward. When at last it crossed the top, two men unhooked the horses and started immediately back toward the camp, the others following and helping drag the heavy singletrees and doubletrees along. There seemed to be no time to rest, for once at the bottom they went to work immediately hooking up another wagon. Yet they were every one cold, every one thoroughly soaked and up to their knees in the wet, still-falling snow, and every one was absolutely exhausted.

"I can't believe this," the driver muttered as he gazed about him. "I'd freeze to death!"

"Some thought they would, though actually not one of them did. Still, there *were* accidents."

"I'll bet! I would think . . . Hey, look at that!"

The driver stared as a wagon broke loose from its chains, rolled backward down the steep hill, and turned over with its tongue sticking up into the air. The men scrambled down to the wreckage and tore the wagon down, and within minutes they were carrying the parts up the grade so that the wagon could be reassembled on top.

"Can you believe that?" the driver declared. "I'll bet they didn't waste two minutes!"

"No, but it has happened before, so they know exactly what to do. Just yesterday Sister Decker, who is working over there by that fire, rolled her wagon."

"She doesn't look hurt."

"No, but both she and her baby girl might have been if the Lord had not been protecting them. She drove the wagon up a steep sidehill below here. A horse crowded the wagon off the grade, and it rolled, breaking all the dishes and everything else that was breakable in the wagon. Sister Decker was thrown free, and her baby, rolled up in a feather bed for warmth, was unhurt as well."

"They were lucky."

"Some would call it that, but such do not have an eternal perspective. Have you noticed the rock ledges in the bottom of the ravine?"

"No, I . . . Wait a minute! That's right! There are grooves in them, cable grooves. I've always thought these people used cable. In fact, the cable wore grooves into the rock three and four inches deep. Those grooves are still there in those ledges! I've seen them."

"Yes," the old man agreed. "They are, but they were not made by this first group. The cable will be used later, when this becomes the road from the mission back to the settlements."

"You . . . you mean they used this road more than once?"

"Of course. The road will be used for almost two years. In fact, at the top of Cottonwood Canyon, near where you parked your jeep, if you had looked off to the left perhaps fifty feet, you would have found a large roll of that old cable still hidden under a rock overhang. It will be left there after this road is abandoned, and it will never be retrieved."

"Without cable," the driver said thoughtfully. "I

can hardly believe it. These poor folks really had to
work their hearts out, didn't they."

"People settling a new land work very hard
whenever they need to go anywhere. Whether the
grade is up or down, it will never be easy."

"Nothing is easy for any of us," the driver replied.

"That is so, my son, especially for you."

"What do you mean?"

"Your way down has not been easy at all, for you
knew too much of the things of eternity. Yet you
have worked hard at it, you have chipped and hammered and drilled at the Spirit of the Lord until it
has fallen away. You have wrapped the cable of
selfishness around your heart until you have become deadened to the spirit of Christ, and at last
you have succeeded in destroying yourself."

"Now wait just a cotton-picking—"

But the old man was already holding his dipper
in the air.

*"I don't know, young feller. The wife and I already
have insurance, and we ain't never had no trouble with
them folks who sold it to us."*

*"Of course you haven't," the salesman agreed, his voice
soft and easy. "Why should you have trouble? You've been
paying them probably twice what that insurance is worth,
and they'd like all that money to continue. Why should they
give you trouble? Besides, have you ever had a claim?"*

"Well, no, but—"

*"Take my word for it, folks. If you ever have a claim,
no matter how big or small it is, that company will give you
nothing but grief. If you ever have a claim, then you will
find out what trouble is."*

"Hold on," the old farmer growled. "Are you telling me, young feller, that we've been took?"

The salesman spread his hands, palms down, and smiled. "What can I say? I don't like to put down another company, folks, but I guess the best word for what you have been through is robbery."

"Can you prove that?"

"Of course I can. Just tell me the amount of your monthly premium, and I—"

"We pay annually. We're farmers, you know."

Quickly the salesman smiled. "Of course you are," he agreed. "I was just testing you to see if you remembered." He waited through their brief smile. "Now what was it you said your annual premium amounted to?"

The elderly farmer told him, and quickly the salesman got out his tables and his calculator. His competitor's rate was good, he thought as he worked his calculator keys, better even than his with the same benefits.

Still, some of those benefits were unnecessary for this old couple. For instance, on the old man's property insurance, the present-value replacement rider could easily be eliminated, as could the fire coverage for all the outbuildings. Of course the old farmer needn't know about that, just as he needn't know about the balloon premium that would be tacked onto his life policy. After all, it wouldn't come due for five years, and by then these old folks would likely be long gone. And for sure he himself would, the salesman thought with a mental grin.

So he could sell the policy that had the most strict exclusions and limitations, and these sorry souls would never know what had been taken from them. And most likely, it would never matter at all.

Of course, in the strictest sense of the word, the omissions he was considering were unethical and maybe even illegal. But Jeannie's new car and that boat on Lake Powell were expensive. Jan was beginning to want a new outfit for every week of school. All Bryan's friends had ATCs, all-terrain cycles, and he wanted one too. The list went on and on. Besides that, he had hardly anything put away in Bryan's missionary fund. No sir, it wasn't easy getting along any more.

Of course, he could feel his conscience nagging at him a bit, but it shouldn't, taking into consideration that he knew more about a family's insurance needs than these two old folks ever would. Why, in years to come they'd probably thank him for saving them that huge premium. Besides, the odds of them having a claim in the next few years were a hundred to one. That was why insurance was such a good business.

Mentally the salesman grinned again, this time thinking of his boss's favorite saying. "These days," his boss said at least once a week, "a man does either what he is born to, what he is used to, or what he has to." In the driver's case, the first one didn't count, and the third one was making the second one more easy. Simple, once a man got the picture of where he was going. Selling these old folks was simply doing what he had to do.

"Folks," he said easily as he lifted his eyes up from his calculator, "I can cut your premium by about . . . let me see here . . . yes . . . by about . . . fifty percent."

"Fifty percent?"

"Absolutely. Here are the figures, right here."

"Our benefits stay the same?"

"Essentially, yes."

"Essentially? What does that mean?"

"Well, you know, every policy's a little different; a few dollars more here, a few dollars less there. Still, the policies are basically the same. If you'd like, I'd be happy to take three or four hours and explain the ramifications and parameters of my policy to you. Or, we can just sign you up, I can get out of your hair, and when the policy comes you can read through it and give me a call if you have any questions.

"Do you have several more hours tonight, or would you rather wait and do it at your leisure?"

The old couple looked at each other, hesitated, and then looked back at the salesman. "And you say our premium is cut by half?" the man asked. "And our benefits stay about the same?" his wife added.

"Half, and the same," the salesman answered, smiling. "Now, if you'll sign right here . . ."

"My son," the old man asked quietly, "do you see how hard you worked to destroy your conscience?"

"Now just a minute, old man! You saw my thoughts just as clearly as I did. I *needed* that sale, and all the others I made, too. It was a matter of survival. Besides, I was doing those old folks a favor, saving them money. I know insurance, I know what people need, and that's what I sell them. What they need! I make money, they save money. No one is hurt, everyone is blessed. How can that be destroying my conscience?"

The old man did not answer, but lifted his arm again—

And the salesman found himself watching the old couple standing in tears watching their home burn. Of course it had been insured, but the salesman watched as they discovered that their furnishings were covered only at used value rather than replacement value, watched as the stress of not being able to afford even the little things of life ate at them and destroyed their health, watched as the balloon premium notice came to them in the mail, watched as the old man, up late pacing the floor with worry, died from a heart attack, watched as the old woman, suddenly alone, discovered that the coverage on her husband's life was only a few thousand dollars, watched as—

"Wait!"

"But why?" the old man asked gently.

"I . . . I've seen enough. Besides, I . . . I didn't know . . ."

"You knew, my son. You knew. Behold."

————————

"Homer, for crying out loud, you've got to get your act together!"

Homer Bean smiled. "Hey, I'm doing fine."

"Yeah, sure," the salesman declared. "Fine as in driving a beat-up Volks, fine as in starving, fine as in failing. Don't you ever want to get ahead in this business?"

"I'm getting ahead," Homer Bean answered amiably. "The Lord has blessed me more than I can imagine. Ever since I was called into the bishopric, the sales just keep coming in."

"Sure they do, like a dried-up stream. Homer, if you'd just listen to me, I could show you how to double, even triple your volume."

"All right, I'm listening."

"Good! Now remember when we had our orientation meetings down in Dallas? Remember how old Turnbudge told us to make our presentations, talking for an hour and half about a fifty-thousand-dollar policy, then quoting them a ten-thousand-dollar policy premium? Of course, you tell the client what you've done, but they've got fifty thousand so firmly planted in their minds that fifty thousand is all they're thinking. So boom, you've got the sale because they think they're getting such a good deal. That's one way."

"You're right," Homer Bean responded quietly, "that is one way."

"You do that, Homer, and you'll pick up volume. But I'll tell you another way, and it works even better."

"I don't think I want to hear it."

"*Sure you do. Wouldn't you like to see Ann and all those kids in a new car? Wouldn't it be nice if you had more bedrooms, or, even better, wouldn't you love to see your family in a newer and larger home? Come on, Homer, be reasonable.* Everybody does it.*"*

"*I don't,*" *Homer said quietly.* "*It's wrong, and I won't be a part of any of it!*"

"*Well, that cuts it!*" *the driver declared, using his facial expression as well as his voice to show his disgust.* "*I'm through trying to help you out. I look at Ann and your poor kids and I ache! They don't have anything! Homer, you ought to be ashamed! Why live in poverty when you don't have to? Why turn your back on good deals when they're all around you for the taking? I'll tell you something. I don't understand you at all.*"

"*Nor I you,*" *Homer said quietly.* "*Here we are in the Lord's church; we both have testimonies, we are both leaders, and yet you act as though you don't even care what Christ taught.*"

"*I care, Homer. I'm just realistic about this world He has sent us to live in.*"

"*No, you are blind about it.*"

"*Hey, you're the one who told me I had learned to be a king in the preexistence. I'm just being a king!*"

"*Yes, and I also told you that since that was the case, in this life you were to work on priestly or spiritual attitudes and behavior. You're not only not working on them, you've killed them! I ache because of your spiritual blindness.*"

"*We'll see who is blind,*" *the salesman declared.* "*We'll see who really aches for whom. We'll also see whom the Lord blesses and prospers, you and your mamby-pamby do-gooder approach to business, or me with my natural, incisive talents. Do you remember the scripture in 1 Timothy where Paul calls us infidels and deniers of the faith if we don't properly provide for our children? What about that, Homer? Huh? What about it?*"

"*Yes, Paul said it,*" *Homer agreed.* "*But in the sixty-*

83

eighth section of the Doctrine and Covenants, in verses 25 through 28, the Lord clarifies all those other statements by declaring that such providing was to be in the way of proper teaching and example as well as anything else. How can you be setting the proper example for Jeannie, Jan, and Bryan when your heart is set so much on the things of this world and you are aspiring so strongly for the honors of men that you have forgotten the Lord?"

"Forgotten the Lord?" the salesman laughed. "We'll see who rises fastest in this company, and then we'll know who has his head on most straight and who has forgotten the Lord!"

84

"What does success in the insurance industry have to do with things eternal?" Homer asked sadly. And then, without waiting for an answer, he continued. "My friend, the tragedy of all this is that with all your God-given talents and abilities, you have no idea what you are about. For some reason you equate 'business' with getting; you equate 'success' with acquiring. True business and true success have little to do with getting and acquiring. Those two things are merely by-products, and they come as they are needed to the truly successful businessman."

"And I suppose you know what true business success is?" the salesman asked sarcastically.

"I do. A truly successful businessman is one who diligently strives to serve others."

"Serve? Good grief, man, what do you think I do? I'm always serving clients."

"Are you?" Homer Bean quietly questioned. "Does one who serves cheat and steal? Does he misrepresent his product or his company? Come on, brother, think about it. Business is the art of blessing other people's lives, and of being honestly rewarded for those blessings. After all, the greatest businessman of all is God, and His whole focus is to bless us, His children. He is then paid, if you will, by our obedience, as far as we can pay him. If you want to be a truly successful businessman, forget those sorry jerks in Dallas

and elsewhere. Pattern your business methods after God's, and you will make it."

"Oh sure! And I suppose you think that's what you do?"

"No, but I try. Every day I try."

"You still don't understand," the salesman responded emphatically. *"God gave me certain talents; I am using them, and the faster I get ahead, the sooner I will be able to get out of this rat race and give all my time to serving God. I'll tell you what, very soon I will be well enough off that I can leave for three years and serve as a mission president. I'll do it, too, and I'll be a good one. Beyond that, who knows?*

"Look at Tom Bird. He was called to be a mission president last year. He's about thirty-five, wealthy, and retired. Do you think he got there by using emotion and love to make every decision? You can bet your sweet booties he didn't! Face it. He's a realist, and look how the Lord has blessed him."

"I can tell that you don't know Tom Bird," Homer Bean responded.

"I do! All I have to do is look at him and I know him."

"Then you know that Tom was never in business as such, but was a seminary teacher."

"Well," the salesman said as he hesitated, *"whatever he was, if I just keep going, in another year or so my time will be mine, just as Tom Bird's is, and then the Lord can use me in any way He chooses. He knows that, and that's why He is blessing me with so much success. I just wish you'd be more open to His help, because I think the Lord is working through me to try to help you."*

Homer Bean looked long into his friend's eyes, and at last he shook his head in absolute bewilderment. *"Tom Bird was honest,"* he declared. *"But you* hurt *people! How can you possibly feel righteous enough to become a mission president when you hurt people?"*

"Hurt people? Homer, you are so naive. I never hurt a

soul in my life. I give them what they want; they pay for what they get. How can that be unrighteous? How can it hurt them? In fact, my methods are the ultimate in honesty, because they make people face reality. Now, are you willing to let me teach you?"

Homer Bean stared at the salesman. His heart ached because he could not communicate his message, and sadly then he shook his head once more.

The Grappling

"Once again your best friend couldn't get through to your conscience," the old man said as he and the driver stood in a driving blizzard at the top of the Slick Rocks, a location they had just reached.

"That's because he was wrong!" the driver declared as he stared at the pioneers below him. "He was wrong then, and he still is! Hurt people! How ridiculous. I just wish—What . . . what are these poor, miserable pioneers doing now?"

"Getting down from Gray Mesa. Their scouts got up here and couldn't find a way off. Then George Hobbs, out hunting a trail, followed a mountain sheep, and suddenly he realized that he had been led down from the mesa."

"Probably thinks the Lord sent the sheep, doesn't he."

"He says he does," the old man replied. "That way, whether Father was involved or not, Brother Hobbs and the others will be blessed for giving God the honor and the glory. Such faith is a part of earning blessings."

"And of course this cliff is the way that sheep

went down? I've hiked it, old man, and the trail is pathetic."

"Yes, but this slick-rock bulge is nowhere near as bad as the Hole-in-the-Rock. Still, they have been here for several days, cutting horizontal grooves into the rock and filling them with sand so that the animals and themselves will have footing. They have also had to blast out two separate dugways, and you can see that they are both quite steep."

"There are cable grooves here too."

"Yes, but as I told you, cables are not being used by this first group. Once again, those grooves will be made by later travelers. Notice how that wagon is being lowered with drag logs and the animals in front are holding it back? That is how it will need to be done with each of the eighty-two wagons in the train."

"I thought there were eighty-three."

"There were, but one has been abandoned because it has been so severely damaged. Once the wagons are down, the thousand and some head of livestock have to be led down the same precipitous trail, which is being made even more treacherous by the snow and ice. Down below they've chipped those two dugways out of the rock, and by nightfall the entire train should be at the bottom."

"In this blizzard?" the driver asked, wondering with part of his mind why he did not feel the cold.

"Oh, yes. They don't have time to wait for good weather. Their food is running low, they are months late, and they must get on their way to Montezuma Fort."

"But they . . . they . . . some of them will never make it! This rock is slick. Somebody will be killed before today is over."

"No," the old man argued, "no one will be hurt.

In fact, no one will die during the entire expedition. Most of them, Mormons and non-Mormons alike, have great faith, and the Lord is protecting *all* of them."

"It . . . it must have been a miserable trip."

"Thus far," the old man responded, "it has been. Still, all of them do their best to be happy. Sammy Cox, their 'fiddler in buckskin pants,' has done much to help. He is a carefree soul, and is ever a tonic and salve to the tired bodies and spirits of the others."

"Is he here?"

"Oh, yes. Right now he is helping the Holyoaks get their wagon down the lowest dugway. He loves to help others. Tonight, after the blizzard, he will do a little fiddling, Ben and Hyrum Perkins will do a few of their snappy Welsh jigs, and then Ben will throw a few rhythmical snatches to the others. Before long they will all be dancing around their hard-gathered shadscale fires, doing Scotch Reels, Virginia Reels, schottisches, polkas, and even stately minuets."

"You make this sound like it was fun."

"For some, perhaps it is. Still, they are all enduring great trials, and in years to come most will be unable to speak of this journey without shedding a few tears. In fact, since we speak of trials, do you see that wagon back there that has been pulled off the trail?"

"Yes, I see it."

"Sister Olivia Larson, up there on the wagon seat, is preparing to give birth this afternoon. However, the wagon is not adequate for her needs, so her husband, Mons, is trying to pitch that tent."

"He's not having much luck."

"No. The winds are too strong, and the others do not know of his plight. He will finally get the tent up, but in the meantime Sister Larson will have given birth to her son John Rio while she is lying on the spring seat of that wagon."

"You mean out in front of the cover? In this weather?"

"Of course. It is where she is."

"But . . . but why didn't anyone help?"

"Apparently they don't know, but—Good! Do you see them now? There come Seraphine Decker and Jim Decker to help. Look how she is running ahead of him! She *knows* about giving birth. The baby has already come, of course, but they will help get Sister Larson into the tent and do what they can for her there."

"And she will be all right?"

"Of course she will. In just four days she will be walking and working right alongside the other women."

The driver shook his head, then reached down and picked up a small round stone that was lying where the wind had swept the rock free of snow.

"Have you ever noticed these rock marbles?" he asked.

"I have."

"I've often wondered how they got here."

"They were created in volcanic fire centuries ago. Below us are many more of them, and one day a spring near here will be known by the cowboys as Marble Camp. Throw the stone over the edge."

The driver tossed the stone and watched it roll down the steep snow-covered slope. At first it rolled freely, but then snow began to cling to it. It gathered more snow, and soon the tiny stone marble had become a huge snowball.

"Do you see?" the old man asked. "Do you see how the snow built up around the stone as it rolled down?"

"I see. And so what? I've done that hundreds of times."

"Good," the old man responded. "It has been much the same with the deeds of your life. As you have rolled downward you have carried them with you, never shedding them through repentance, and now the weight of them has grown until it is almost impossible for you to turn back toward the truth."

"Oh, come off it," the driver growled. "These degrading remarks aren't really necessary, you know. You took advantage of my weakness because of loss of water; you drugged me so that I am seeing these crazy visions; and now you preach to me as well. Old man, I'm getting sick of it, and sick of you! When this drug wears off I'm going to—"

"Hurt more people? Of course you won't, for you have given me your shadow."

"I'm telling you, I never hurt anyone! I never—"

But the old man wasn't listening. Instead his arm was in the air once more, the dipper tipped to the side—

"His claim is how big?" the salesman asked with astonishment.

"Three and a half million dollars," the claims adjuster replied. "Do you have any idea what that will do to AMPAX if we have to pay? Do you have any idea what that will do to you?"

The salesman shook his head in disbelief and watched the adjuster walk away. Then quickly he turned toward his files, suddenly very concerned about that policy. After all, if he had written it so that AMPAX was liable and the big boys upstairs found out—

The ringing of the phone spun him about, but with customary brightness he lifted the receiver.

"AMPAX. Yes. Hey, how are you, Jim?"

The salesman listened briefly, winked at his secretary, and then broke into the man's conversation. "Okay, Jim, give it to me again so I can get it all down. You've been done out of three and a half million. The guy who took it was an employee you had fired. In retaliation he stole your stocks, bonds, and cash, and then he burned down every haystack and outbuilding on your place? No kidding? Well, it might have been worse. He might have burned down your home . . . He did? You're kidding! How could he possibly have got the water through that silage bin and into your home? That's really too bad. So the home is flooded and destroyed as well? Jim, that's terrible! I . . . Well, I was just reaching for your file when you called. I haven't had . . . Jim, I know we've been best friends for years. Yes, I . . . well, if I told you that, then you can bank on it. No, I . . . listen, don't pay attention to those clowns from our claims division. I'll get your file out, and then we'll be in touch. Meanwhile, look at the bright side of things. At least you don't have to milk the cows."

The salesman laughed at his little joke, said good-bye, set the phone down, and reached for the file.

"I hope we don't find what you are looking for," a voice said from behind him.

Turning, the salesman was surprised to find the regional representative standing before his desk.

"Hi, Fred," he said easily. "I was just getting out the Scranton file."

"I know."

"Then maybe I missed something? What do you hope that I don't find?"

"For your sake I hope we don't find that you blew it," Fred replied. "I've pulled James Scranton's payment data from the computer, and for the premium he's been paying, he can't be covered on any of the stuff he's lost."

"I just told him I didn't think he was," the salesman replied. "When I sold him the policy he was in a cash bind, so

we eliminated a few items from his coverage so that we could get the premium down. As I remember, theft and fire and flooding were some of the things that got cut."

"Why don't you go through the file right now?"

Hastily the salesman complied. "Okay," he said moments later, "here it is, in the fine print. Scranton has full coverage except for these minor exclusions: fire, floods, theft, wind, and vandalism."

"Not much of a policy you sold him, was it," the regional representative stated.

The salesman grinned. "I guess we all get what we pay for, don't we."

"Seems like it. You going to call Scranton and tell him?"

"Uh . . . probably not. I think I'll let my secretary do it."

"Let her take the heat, huh?"

"Hey, why should there be heat? He had a copy of the policy. I told him to read it and call me if he had questions. In fact, while we were cutting the premiums I'm sure I told him which exclusions he was picking up. See here? Take a look at this! Here is Scranton's signature, right below the list of exclusions!"

The two men grinned at that. Fred walked away, and the salesman sat there with his hands clasped behind his head, thinking of—

"You didn't tell Jim Scranton any of that, did you."

The salesman spun around and found Homer Bean staring at him. "Hey, Homer," he smiled, "what are you doing at this office?"

"Seeing you," Homer Bean replied. "Jim Scranton called me on the phone—"

"Why you? I'm his agent."

"Maybe, but I'm in his bishopric, remember. Are you aware that this will force a good man into bankruptcy? Are you aware that with his wife's bad health it very well might kill her? Are you aware that the ward will have to take over

his son's mission expenses? Are you aware, most of all, that Jim Scranton considers you to be one of his best friends, you who have destroyed everything he ever had."

"Homer," the salesman responded, rising to his feet, "I don't have to take this from you! Not you or anybody else."

"You're going to take it from me," Homer Bean replied forcefully. "Jim Scranton trusted you, and now you've destroyed him!"

"Homer," the surprised salesman responded, "I didn't destroy anything! Jim Scranton is a big boy, just like everybody else. He knows you don't get something for nothing. When I cut his premium I saved him big bucks, and that is what he wanted. That boy's mission was coming up, and Jim told me he needed money to send his son out. I gave him that money through lower premiums. If he'd wanted to pay more, I'd have written more coverage. It was Jim's choice, not mine."

"But he didn't know about that choice!"

"I didn't say that, Homer. I have a distinct memory of telling him every item that we cut while we were cutting his premium. I've got his signature right here to prove it."

"Isn't it strange that Jim has a distinct memory too, one that remembers only all the things you promised him?"

The salesman grinned. "The memories of some people are better than others. Besides, I'm sure your memory would change too, if you had three and a half million dollars at stake."

Angrily Homer Bean moved toward the salesman, but then with a mighty effort he turned himself away. "My friend," he said through gritted teeth, "I feel sorry for you. I feel sorry that you could help destroy a good man and be so calloused about it. I feel sorry that you could unconscionably twist things so that Jim Scranton appears to be the bad guy, when you and I both know who it really is! I feel . . . I feel . . . I ache because I am so afraid for your eternal destiny."

"Hey, Brother Bean, don't you be afraid for me! I'm going straight to the top, and when I get there—"

"And you still say your actions have not hurt people?" the old man questioned softly.

The two stood together on a shelf below the rim of a slick-rock mesa. There was snow about. The wind howled past them, and the driver found part of his mind wondering once again why he did not feel the cold. The other part of his mind, however, the busy part, was going over what he had just seen, just hallucinated, just remembered.

He had almost forgotten about Scranton, it had been so long ago. He'd heard from somebody, however, that he was in a rest home somewhere. After his wife had died, he'd—

"Was he not hurt? Was his wife not hurt?"

"Sure he was hurt," the driver mumbled. "But it was his own fault, his and hers. They had the policy. They should have read it."

"And all the other clients you have hurt?"

"What others? There were no others."

"Would you like to see each one?" the old man asked.

The driver, pulling fearfully back against the rock, shook his head. "Maybe some got hurt," he admitted then, "but that is business, pure and simple. Buyer beware, I think the motto is. The buyers have the responsibility to find out what they are buying before they buy it. That's why we have contracts, you know. So the client can see what he's getting. Every policy I sell tells my client exactly what he is getting, and the way I see things, it is the client's responsibility if he doesn't read his policy."

"And your responsibility?"

"Just myself," the driver said with finality. "Myself and my family."

"Look below you," the old man directed. "Tell me what you see."

The driver looked and saw that the wagons of the pioneers, all eighty-two of them, were scattered along the bank of a small, icy stream. The stock were in a ragged herd downstream, foraging for grass through the thin snow. At the camp several fires burned brightly, and a few people worked busily above them. Others lay in blankets beneath the wagons.

"They . . . they are resting," he said, wishing he had not answered but once again knowing that he had no choice.

"That is right. This is called Lake Canyon, for below here is an ancient lake that they called Hermit or Pahragit Lake, where they rested for several days before they came here."

"This is where I couldn't get any seepage last night."

"That is correct."

"Seems to be plenty of water now. You know, I've explored where the lake once was. It's too bad it drained out."

"Yes, but now that these people have moved on, there will be no need for the lake to remain. For the past three days, however, that lake has been the finest camp these tired missionaries have enjoyed thus far. It is very deep. It is almost half a mile long and about that wide. And it is surrounded by cottonwoods, willows, canes, flags, and bulrushes. And amongst all that, several kinds of grasses also grow luxuriantly. There everyone rested, everyone cleaned up in the clear and plentiful water, and the stock rested and fed on the nourishing grasses that the Lord had allowed to grow there.

"Now, however, they are traveling once more. Do you see anything else that might be worthy of note?"

"I don't think they are all here. Some of the men are missing."

"That is correct. Many of the men have gone ahead to work on another stretch of the road. It is hard, cold work, but it must be done. What else do you see?"

"I see a woman down there. But what—"

"Her baby is secured so that his feet are down in the front of her dress against her body. That way the baby's feet and legs will not freeze. If you notice, most women with babies are carrying them that way. They have done so all along, but you have not had eyes to see.

"Of course, as you can also see, the men, women, and children under the wagons are sick. They have endured much illness and will have much more to go through before their journey is at an end. What else do you see?"

The driver turned his head away, desperately trying to keep from saying what he knew would come forth from his mouth. He must not admit it! He must be strong against this evil old man, he must—

"Those w-women," he gasped, at last unable to hold out, "are . . . are feeding all the m . . . men. Some . . . some are carrying babies that are not theirs, keeping them warm, and . . . and . . ."

"Yes?"

"Everyone is . . . is working together; even the children are . . . are helping."

"But how can that be," the old man asked gently,

"when each family's responsibility should be only to itself? Isn't that what you just told me you believed?"

"You don't understand!" the driver cried. "Maybe this helping each other out was the way it used to be when these pioneers or missionaries or whatever you call them were here, but no more! The world today is different! Today it is every man for himself, and the tougher a man is, the better he does.

"If I weren't strong and hard, I'd be a bigger failure, a bigger loser, than Homer Bean! If I didn't take care of my family, no one would! I'm a survivor, and I've done what I had to do so that my family and I could survive! That is the gospel truth, old man, and you can take it to the bank. I know it is true, my wife knows it is true, and we've taught it to our children. We're alone in this crazy world, and so we have to fight for everything we get. That is a fact!"

The old man gazed at the driver and suddenly lifted his dipper into the raging wind. "Behold," he said quietly, and once again the driver was adrift—

98

"Get off!" the boy ordered as he balled his fist into the face of the smaller youth.

The younger boy cringed, but he did not let go of the handlebars of the ATC.

"I said get off! And do it now, before I knock your block off, you little wimp!"

"You can't have it, Bryan," the smaller boy whined fearfully. "It . . . it's my dad's, and he won't let anybody ride it but me. I can't—"

"I warned you," the older boy declared, and he smashed

his fist into the face of the smaller youth. "I'm riding that bike, and no one is going to stop me."

"How . . . how are you doing this?" the driver whispered. "I mean, I haven't seen this, so I can't be remembering it. But that is my son, and—"

"He is doing that sad deed right now," the old man declared. "You are seeing it as it is happening, as it is being recorded for his own future learning."

"But how—"

"Once again, is that so important as why?"

The driver dropped his head. "I . . . I know why, because I can see his thoughts. He thinks that hitting the boy is . . . is what I would do if I were there. But I wouldn't! I'd never—"

"Hurt someone smaller than you?" the old man continued the statement as a question.

"I . . . I . . ."

"My son, do you see now that your selfish philosophy of life has inflicted the greatest hurt on those who love you the most? Are you able at last to see the effects of your dishonesty? Do you see now the manner in which you have given me your shadow?"

His voice filled with desperation, the driver shouted, "I never did any of this intentionally! I wouldn't do that to someone who loves me. Okay, so I've made mistakes. Who hasn't? I'm sorry my boy thinks that way, and when I get back I'll make certain he understands that."

"Your manner of living has affected many others besides your son. What do you intend to do about each of them?"

"Oh, come on," the driver stormed, "I'm not

going to carry the burden for the rotten things every creep in America does. I'm not about to be held accountable for all of that!"

"Not even some of it?" the old man asked gently. "Not even the behavior of those you have personally wounded? Are we not our brother's keepers?"

"Nobody believes in that old nonsense, not today. The world has changed—"

With a wave of his hand the old man lifted the dipper, and instantly the driver was drifting again, and all that he saw condemned him. He saw Homer Bean listening on the telephone as the driver's wife, Jeannie, pleaded with Homer to not give up on her husband. Shocked by that, he saw Homer playing ball with the driver's son, saw him speaking with the driver's clients, actually heard him defending the driver in conversation after conversation with the people to whom the driver had already sold insurance policies.

As he stared in dumbfounded silence, the driver saw others, too, friends and neighbors, Church members and business acquaintances, and he heard their thoughts as they tried to love him and to help him and his family. But mostly he saw Homer Bean, again and again, as he quietly did his best to love the driver and help him learn to love in return.

Yet through it all the driver stood, immovable as a spire of granite, unbending and unyielding in his belief that he was doing right, that he was alone against the world, that he was being the best that he could be in his chosen life and profession.

And then—

"Hiya, sweetheart. How's it going today?"
The salesman watched the young woman's eyes, know-

ing that he could see much there. She liked him, he knew that, liked him even more than she should. But today was not the day for that. Today he hoped only that he could see in her eyes that she would help him.

"Hi," she said sincerely as she turned from her word processor. "I didn't know you were in town today."

"I wasn't supposed to be," he grinned, "but with things coming to a head, I thought, well, what the heck? Might as well go for broke, if you know what I mean."

The driver winked, and the young woman laughed. "You're nervous, aren't you," she said.

"I sure am. Nervous as a chirpie going to church. They've narrowed the field to myself and one other man, and I've got to make certain that the best man wins. And we both *know who that is, don't we."*

Both the salesman and the young woman laughed together then, and as the laughter died away he saw it, saw in the secretary's eyes the desire to please him, a desire that would take her to almost any length he asked. That was when he knew that he had won.

"How does it look?" he asked quietly, sincerely.

"The truth?"

"The truth."

"Well, not very good, at least for you. It's pretty close for everything but sales totals, and there your competition really edges you out."

The driver stared at the floor, his mind racing. How could that be? How could a man like Homer possibly have more sales than himself?

"Are you sure?" he asked.

"Absolutely. Not only is he doing better, but the agents under him have really been pushing things. You wouldn't believe their volume."

It figures, the salesman thought. *That man always could make people feel sorry for him. And that had to be how he was doing it.*

"Do you know the other man?" he asked.

"I don't. I can't even remember his name."

"Homer Bean."

"Oh, that's right. I saw the file on him. He has nine children. Can you believe that? His oldest girl is in college. He has one son on a mission or something for the Mormon Church and another ready to go, and the file says he has been made a bishopric, I think. Do you know what that means?"

The salesman laughed. "Sure I do. He's in a bishopric, which means he is one of the counselors to a man who is in charge of a Mormon ward. In other words, he's a yes man."

The secretary looked up at him. "That's not very good, is it? I mean, if he's being considered for the position of regional representative and all—"

"Actually," the salesman said, choosing his words carefully and keeping his voice low so that the girl would feel that she was in on private information, "that is why I came in today. I'm very concerned, and after much thought, I decided this morning that you were the one I should come to for help."

"Well," the young woman replied, lowering her own voice, "you know I'll help you in any way I can. After all, no one else sends me roses once a week. Even my husband doesn't do that."

"He just doesn't know the prize he has," the salesman smiled.

The young woman smiled in return, a warm, intimate smile, and the salesman plunged ahead. "You should know that Homer and I are old friends," he said quietly. "He is a good man, and I think the world of him."

"Uh-huh."

"That is why I came to you. You see, I know him well enough to know that he will not be good for AMPAX as a regional rep, nor will that position be good for him. Of course, I don't really care who gets the position, and I certainly don't want it very badly myself. I mean, who likes to pile pressures upon his own head?"

The young woman laughed, and the driver continued. "*Unfortunately, the position is now between Homer and me, and to prevent him from destroying AMPAX with his weak leadership and other serious problems and ending up getting fired and being unemployed, which would also destroy him, I've got to ensure my own nomination as regional representative.*"

"*But . . . how can you do that?*"

"*Joyce darling, that's where you come in. I need the names of half a dozen of Homer's biggest clients, as well as the yearly premium figures for each of them.*"

"*But I can't—*"

103

"*Don't say you can't until you know why I'm asking. I hate to say this, and you must promise that you will never spread it around. Promise?*"

"*All right.*"

"*Good. My friend Homer Bean, much as I like him, is nothing more than a cheat and a thief.*"

"*Really?*"

"*Absolutely. That's why we have to do this. To save him from himself and AMPAX from him as well, here is what I propose to do about it. I'll go to Homer's biggest clients, show them how I can lower their premiums for the same coverage—*"

"*But can you do that?*"

"*Of course I can. Homer is always gouging his clients, and no matter how I've tried to talk to him about it, he keeps it up. I guess with all those kids he just needs more money than he can honestly earn. Anyway, I'll show his clients how much I can save them, then have them write letters to the boys upstairs saying how much more efficient and wonderful and macho and all that stuff I am—*"

The young woman giggled.

"*All I need,*" *the salesman continued,* "*is that tiny bit of data, and we will be on our way.*"

"*But I can't . . . I mean, I'm not supposed to—*"

"*Now I know there is a risk in this,*" *the salesman said, interrupting her and lowering his voice even more.* "*But I am more than willing to make it worthwhile for you. After I am nominated, and I will be if you can get me that data, you will automatically become my personal secretary, and I will guarantee you at least a fifty percent raise."*

"F-fifty percent?"

"That's right. Half again what you are making now."

The secretary's eyes grew big as she mentally worked out the amount of her new salary. "And you promise you won't tell anybody?" she asked hesitantly.

"Hey, who would I tell? Myself? Remember, I'd be boss then, so neither of us would have anything to worry about. But more important than your salary and my position would be the fact that you and I, together, have, first, saved AMPAX from the tragedy of an inept leader, and, second, saved Homer and his large family from the tragedy of unemployment."

"You're right," the girl said quietly as she stared into the screen of the word processor. "You're right. We really do need to help the poor man. Very well, for you and AMPAX and your friend and all those kids of his I will do it. But I wouldn't want you to think I was doing this just because you've promised me more money."

"Oh no, I don't think that at all."

"Good, because I don't care about the money. Really, I don't. In fact, I don't think I want the raise."

"Well, we can talk about that later, if you'd like."

"There's no need to. I really don't want it. Still, I can get that data for you this afternoon. Where can I meet you?"

"Rori's Diner, on the corner of Michelle and Monica streets."

"Great. I'll see you there at five. And remember, mum's the word."

"Hey, sweetheart," the salesman grinned, "mum about what? I haven't the faintest idea what you're talking about."

He winked then, the young woman winked in return,

and the salesman walked easily from the office, the position of regional representative virtually his.

The driver stared with eyes that didn't want to see; he ached in his heart with a hollow emptiness that grew worse with each parading scene; he heard his thoughts as he went through client after client with his glib tongue and lying words; he heard himself laugh inwardly as Homer Bean tried to be his friend; he heard his lies as he stole the regional representative position from Homer—

105

"There is a chill in the air," the old man said as he placed several sticks in the small fire.

The driver started, for suddenly they were back at the camp in Wilson Canyon near Mormon Wells. There had been no sense of moving, no feeling that he was traveling. Only somehow he had come all the way from Lake Powell on the south, or at least he had come all the way from where Lake Powell now lay, and had traveled far to the north, all the way to Lake Canyon. But it was again hot, terribly hot. Only . . . only seconds ago he had been in the midst of snow and cold and the rock and those miserable missionary pioneers who had spent over six months of their lives crawling through this horrible wilderness.

But why . . . how . . .

And then it came to him, the answer to all the questions he had asked himself a hundred times as he had climbed and driven the torturous trail from Cottonwood Canyon to Clay Hill Pass and on to San Juan Hill. Now he understood not only how those old Hole-in-the-Rock missionaries had done it, but why.

And the why? Simply because they had had the

faith needed to be obedient even when it was difficult to be so. As for the how, it was because for the most part they had worked together, had sustained each other's beliefs, had lifted each other's spirits, and had moved forward *together*. They had been human, yes, and so had made mistakes. But they had managed through general selflessness to overcome much of the weakness of the flesh, and they had looked with mostly forgiving hearts upon each other for almost the entire rugged trek.

Now the driver could see how wrong he had been! Now he could see what Homer had been trying all these years to teach him! It was that men got furthest ahead in life by helping each other.

"Old man," he said as he stared at the shadowy figure across the fire, "may I . . . may I ask you a question?"

"Of course."

"Was this to teach me? Was this whole miserable experience to help me see my life so that I could go back and change?"

"Partly, perhaps."

"Well, I hope so. I'll tell you this, it has certainly worked. I didn't even know I needed to change, and now I can hardly wait to get about it.

"You know, I have wondered about these pioneers for years, and now their lives have become shining examples for me. Now I know why I have so loved to come into this desert. It is because of them, because of what my soul was hungering to learn from them about human togetherness, about integrity, about obedience. Now I can't wait to get back, I can't wait to begin to undo all the unpleasantness, all the dishonesty, all the pain—"

"My son, you are not going back."

"What? But I thought . . . What about Homer? What about . . ."

106

"The Lord has already taken care of Homer Bean."

"But . . . but there are others! I need to—"

"The damage has been too great, my son. Because of that, it is far too late for you to repent during mortality. Thus I have been sent as the whirlwind to reap you down."

"It's never too late!" the driver shouted. "I can repent! I know I can. I've taught that to people for years. I just need to get back to my jeep. I just . . . What . . . what did you mean, as the whirlwind? Or reap me down? What . . . who . . . who are you?"

"I told you, I was called by the old ones who lived on this land, Taker of Shadows."

"But now? Do you have a name now?"

"I do," the old man answered gently, "and with the revealing of it, you will understand. I am called a Destroyer, an Angel of Destruction. I am sent from the Father, along with hosts of others, to reap down the tares, to separate them from the wheat so that the wheat might be gathered cleanly at the final harvest."

The old man paused and then breathed deeply. "My son," he finally continued, "you have given me your shadow, and so you have been reaped with the tares."

The Escape

The driver stared into the flames of the small fire in the bottom of Wilson Canyon, once again seeing himself as the student, the salesman, the liar, the thief. The images were self-serving, dishonest, and ugly, and he was wracked with incredible guilt and horror that he had been and was still viewing himself and his past.

"No more," he pleaded into the darkness where the old man still sat. "Please, no more."

But the images continued, and the driver's guilt was harrowed up even more. How had he let such things happen to himself? After he had been given so much light and knowledge, why had he allowed himself to turn from it and go the other way? Why—

"Oh, dear Father in heaven," his mind cried out while the images paraded before his eyes, "if only I had listened to thy Spirit, if only I had listened to Homer. I see now that he was always a true friend, and I am so sorry that I did what I did to him! Please forgive me. Please allow *him* to forgive me! Help my children too, and all those others I have injured.

"Dear God, if only I had turned back when there

was time. If I had done that, if I had turned away from darkness and into the light, then perhaps—"

A coyote yipped out on the mesa, and again the driver thought of his wife and family. How could they get along without him? They would do it, he knew that, but how? And what would they think about his disappearance? It might be months before anyone found the jeep. Beyond that, it would be forever before anyone discovered what had happened to him. Why, even he himself didn't understand—

The old man across the fire sighed with deep regret. "My son," he said from the darkness, "it is too late, far too late for such thoughts. Now come, we must be going, for we have centuries of learning ahead of us."

"Centuries? But—"

"I am certain that, for you, it will take that long. But do not fear, for I will guide you through it. Father loves you, and there is redemption for all those who are willing to repent and to learn."

"But that doesn't make sense," the driver cried out in anguish. "I have already changed! Can't you see that? I have learned, and I have the right to go back so that I can prove it!"

"My son, you have no right now but to come with me and since you have given me your shadow, I will teach you."

"No!" the driver screamed. "Nooo! You don't understand! I don't deserve this! I have done many good things in my life! I have helped others; I have tried to be a good father and husband; I brought many people into the Church; I've done all *kinds* of good things. All I've ever wanted to do is get ahead so that I could bless my family. Let me go back!"

"I cannot."

"But why? Why *this?* What is wrong with getting ahead?"

"One last time I will repeat myself. It isn't wanting to get ahead that is wrong, but why you want to. You have no concern for the rest of God's children, and that is why you have given me your shadow."

"Shadow! Shadow! *Shadow!*" the driver shouted in fearful frustration. "What does my shadow have to do with what you are doing to me?"

"Everything," the old man responded. "When you kept the commandments of God, your face was always to His light, the shadow of your soul always behind you, and so your vision of eternal things was never obscured. But then you began turning away from His light, your spiritual shadow moved slowly from behind you, and today when at last it was before you, obscuring your vision of things eternal, I took it unto myself and so have reaped you down."

The driver stared, almost unable to believe, almost unable to comprehend the magnitude of what the old man was saying. But of course, now that he thought of it, the old man was right! It was the light! Of course, *the light of the gospel!* Of truth! Of Christ! Of God the Father!

With his dishonesty and selfishness he had turned away from the light of God, he had rejected the whispered truths of the Holy Ghost, he had ignored the faithful pleadings of his good friend Homer Bean, he—

And then the driver understood why the old man's face was dark! His own spiritual shadow was obscuring all things spiritual before him!

That was why it had become so hard to tell what was right and what was wrong. It was why he had seen monetary prospering as God's blessing, when in reality it had been further condemnation of his

111

own selfishness and dishonesty. It was why he had been unable to discern the true greatness within the unimpressive looking man called Homer Bean! It was why he had never been able to see the light of the old man's countenance.

The driver, his mind numb and his actions truly no longer his own, found himself rising to his feet before the old man. Only, the old man was suddenly not so old, nor was he clothed in skins. His garments were now shimmering with light, beautiful light that had no color and yet was all colors at once. Yet his face remained dark, for the driver still faced him.

Suddenly the gloriously clad being arose and lifted the dipper into the darkness above him.

And then, with a shout of anger and frustration that he had been so harshly judged when in fact there had been such a great deal of good in his life, the driver lunged at the old man. He willed his eyes to bore into the eyes of destruction that had been hidden in shadow before him, he willed his feet to move through the fire toward this being who had been sent to reap him down, and he willed his hands to grasp the ancient dipper and lift it up so that none of its mysterious water could fall out—

And he found himself instantly turned away, his face and his feet all going opposite to where he had willed himself to go.

"It worked!" his mind screamed with joy. "It *worked,* and now the fearsome countenance of that being is not directly before me!"

With a mighty wrench of his heart, the driver cried out to God, whose light he now must surely be facing; cried out his guilt and his shame and his sorrow, cried out his intention to become as honest as a man could possibly be.

Nor had repentance ever been so sudden, so complete, so thorough. In that instant he promised

God all he had and all he had ever hoped to have. He covenanted that never again would he intentionally sin. He agreed that he would accept all callings and fulfill them joyously. He pledged that he would honor his wife and bring up his children in righteousness and truth. He vowed that he would give the position of regional representative for AMPAX back to Homer Bean. He guaranteed that he would sincerely attempt to right all the wrongs his dishonesty had caused with every one of his clients.

And suddenly from behind him the driver heard a wrenching cry, a wail so filled with grief that his entire body shook, and he almost fell to the earth.

"No," the voice of the old man cried. "Do not do this thing! You are not ready. Please wait with me, or it will take so much longer."

But with supreme, almost superhuman effort the driver willed himself not to look back, not to listen. He willed himself to keep his eyes forward, toward where he hoped were the truthful, selfless things of God.

The Decision

The driver was in his jeep, grinding to a stop on the sandy shelf below the stone tanks of Mormon Wells, deep in Wilson Canyon. In the glare of the desert sunset his mouth was dry and his mind was giddy with dizziness, and for a moment he wondered where he was. As the jeep rocked to a stop and sat hissing steam he took a deep breath, relaxed, and dropped his tired hands from the wheel.

He had made it! Finally, after what had seemed hours—

And then realization came. With a gigantic leap of his heart the truth hit home, and the driver understood what had happened.

He was finally free!

He had escaped from the angel of destruction who had controlled him, and his heart filled with joy and gratitude that it was so. His plan, only half-formed when he had leaped at the old man, had worked! He had stopped the pouring of that evil water. He had thwarted the designs of that strange lord-of-past-sins. He had escaped.

He was free!

For a few seconds the driver's soul burned with

his newfound convictions of integrity, and over and over he repeated the vow that he would never tell another lie, that he would never twist his way through another half-truth, that he would never manipulate others to bring about his own selfish ends, that he would forever lead his family in the way of truth and light, that he would rectify all past dishonest deeds.

"Thank you, Father in heaven," he sobbed with relief. "Thank you for helping me to get away! I swear that from now on I will—"

But then the driver's voice grew still. His eyes opened, and his mind came to grips with the fact that he was indeed in his jeep, parked at the bottom of Wilson Canyon. And he also realized, with a jolting start, that nothing else had happened! Nothing had happened at all!

He had . . . he had *hallucinated* all the things he was even at that moment praying about.

Why, he *had* to have hallucinated them. Now that he thought of it, he knew it was so. Hallucination was the only answer that made any sense. First, the jeep's radiator hadn't stopped hissing even yet, so how could he have been sitting for several hours at a fire up by the tanks?

He couldn't have!

Second, it was still daylight, not dark at all.

Third, he was still thirsty, maybe even more so than ever.

And fourth and finally, the milk jug, still behind him in the jeep, was empty and dry.

Carefully, however, the driver looked around him; carefully he tested the air. No sound but the wind assailed his ears, no smell came to his nose but the odor of wet rock and water. Nowhere was there an old man, nowhere was there a sign of smoke or fire.

Shaking his head in wonderment that his mind could wander so far from reality, the driver finally laughed aloud. Of course he had hallucinated! Of course he had been temporarily out of his mind! In fact, even during his delirium he had known it was so and had tried to tell that fact to his struggling brain.

As for his thoughts about dishonesty and selfishness, why, he had hallucinated those because Homer's criticisms of him had been so much on his mind. And as far as his pitying of poor old Homer was concerned, why, it was simply his love and sorrow for the man that had been made manifest. And that love was still there, he thought ruefully, in spite of the damage that Homer Bean had done to him.

117

But the delirium was over now. He had thought it through, had made his decision, was on his way up in the world, and now his troubled conscience could be at rest. Actually, the problem was not a problem at all, unless it was one of perceptions, of outdated beliefs that had to fall before the understanding of modern thought. Besides, he had known all along what he had been doing with his wise deceptions. In spite of what Homer had tried to tell him, he had known all along what was best for his family, his business, Homer Bean, everything, and all his reason and intelligence now told him that he had been right.

Additionally, he had once again beaten the land. Even without water, even with a broken-down jeep, even with the heat and thirst and hallucination, he had won. No longer would he ever need to feel intimidated by what those old pioneers had done. He himself had done just as much, maybe even more, and best of all, he had done it *alone!*

With another hearty laugh at his victory, the driver took up his empty jug and reached to climb from the jeep. Only, as his eyes fell on his hand and wrist, he felt his breath catch deep within his throat.

He tried to scream but couldn't, and he knew with sudden fearful certainty that he would never scream, never again do anything of his own free will.

For an instant that seemed longer than all eternity he stared at the massive burn on his hand and wrist. And then, finally, with the sheer terror of absolute knowledge activating his vocal cords, he was permitted to scream.

And then he screamed again and again, for the burn upon which he gazed was in the deepest shadow he had ever seen, a shadow so deep he could hardly see through it, a shadow that was growing rapidly before him.

"My son," a voice said softly, sadly from beside him, "I yet walk with you, for now truly you shall learn."

Spinning, the driver found himself beside the brilliant form of a man who stood weeping quietly beside the jeep, his tears falling from the shadow that yet obscured his face.

"Oh, no!" the driver wailed.

"Come, my son," the shadowy form said quietly. "You did not learn, and so now we have even more to do."

"But I cannot see you!" the driver cried in anguish. "I still cannot see you!"

"Of course you cannot, for your shadow is even more firmly before you."

"But . . . but will I ever see your face?" the driver asked tremblingly as he involuntarily took his first halting step away from the jeep.

"In the due time of the Lord."

"What does that mean?"

"My countenance," the being responded, "reflects always the pure love of God, for I am His representative. My face cannot be seen until you accept and radiate to others that same pure love that the Father and His Son have manifested always for you. On the day when the love in my countenance becomes obvious, then you will be free. Now shall we go?"

And so, as the pungent odor of smoke and decayed flesh drifted past him, the driver found himself stumbling outward into the shadows of the gathering darkness, his hands held before him as though he were somehow blind, his parched lips screaming that he *would* change if he could just have one more chance, his steps following with exactness in the footsteps of the great being the old ones had called the Shadow Taker, his dehydrated mortal body staggering off into the hot, dry slick-rock country of San Juan County, Utah.

Epilogue

Behold, he was reading, trying his best to ease his aching heart, trying to understand, *there are many called, but few are chosen. And why are they not chosen? Because their hearts are set so much upon the things of this world, and aspire to the honors of men, that they do not learn this one lesson—that the rights of the priesthood are inseparably connected with the powers of heaven, and that the powers of heaven cannot be controlled nor handled only upon the principles of righteousness.*

He paused in his reading to think of what he had just covered, and he found himself considering the meaning of "things of the world" and "honors of men." He was not uncomfortable with thoughts like that, just pensive, and for him that seemed always a good attitude.

For a moment longer he made mental lists of worldly things and honors and thought again with pain of his friend; then his eyes found their way back to the page of scripture, this time to a different place.

Let thy bowels also be full of charity towards all men, and to the household of faith, and let virtue garnish thy thoughts unceasingly; then shall thy confidence wax strong in the presence of God; and the doctrine of the priesthood shall distil upon thy soul as the dews from heaven. The Holy Ghost shall be thy constant companion, and thy scepter an unchanging scepter of righteousness and truth; and thy dominion shall be an everlasting dominion, and without compulsory means it shall flow unto thee forever and ever.

Again he stopped reading, for again his mind was filled with images. Charity was pure love, and the Lord was specifying that a righteous man must love members and nonmembers of God's kingdom alike. With that and a virtuous heart and mind, the Lord would begin to pour out great blessings that finally ended with celestial power that *was* power because it came to the righteous man freely, without compulsion.

Actually, what he had been reading about was simply the doctrine of Godhood, spelled out so plainly by the Lord that anyone could understand it. Only . . . only that wasn't so, for try as he would, he had never been able to get his friend to understand—to listen.

Sudden tears sprang forth, new tears to follow old ones, and he lowered his head and gave vent to the grief that was always so close to the surface. If only he had been better able to explain! If only he had been closer to the Spirit, so that his words to his friend might have had more power. If only—

"Mr. Bean?"

Homer Bean looked up from the empty desk top, his face a mask of grief and sorrow. "Yes?" he said.

"I . . . I heard they found his body. They say he died of dehydration, and maybe shock from a bad burn on his hand. There was a hole in his jeep's radiator, too, but he was so close to water, so *close!*

You'd think that . . . Anyway, I just wanted to say I'm sorry."

"Thank you," Homer Bean whispered as he did his best to smile. "I'm sorry too. I can't even tell you how sorry I am."

The young woman shifted her feet uncomfortably. "You really loved him, didn't you."

It was a statement, not a question, and Homer Bean nodded in response. "Him, his wife Jeannie, the children; I love them all, and I am so sorry that he is gone. He could have done so much if he had been allowed to stay."

"He . . . well, we talked a little," she replied, "and I could tell that . . . that he thought a lot of you as well."

"I know he did," Homer Bean agreed. "We've been best friends ever since college."

The young woman again shifted her feet. "Well," she said, coughing, "don't forget the meeting you've called for tomorrow at nine."

"Meeting? Oh yes, the one with all the regional managers."

"That's the one."

"I won't forget." Homer Bean watched as the young woman stood fidgeting in the doorway, and with all his heart he hoped she would say what her conscience was telling her to say. She was so efficient, so conscientious, and he felt in his heart that she was a good person. Only—

Quickly he glanced at the papers in the wastebasket, at the computer printout of his top clients and the several letters from them to the just retired regional representative, asking that he, Homer Bean, be removed as their agent in favor of his late friend.

Homer had somehow known what had happened when he had been passed over, and now he felt terrible about the burden his friend must have carried with him at the moment of his death. What an awful experience that must have been for him, to have died in his . . . his sins.

Homer could hardly think the word, and immediately he determined that he must not judge him. After all, there had to have been reasons, and besides, the man had done so much for the Church and his quorum members. No, let the Lord decide what would happen, for judgment was His.

But the young woman who stood before him? Well, perhaps if he could persuade her a little—

"Joyce," he said as he dried his eyes, "sit down, please."

Wonderingly, almost fearfully, the young woman moved to do so.

"Joyce, I think a lot of you. Yet we have a problem, you and I, and I need to ask you a hard question. Okay?"

The young woman nodded slowly, and so Homer Bean continued.

"Joyce, do you have access to private data from the computer?"

"I . . . I . . . well, yes, I can get at a little of it."

"A little?"

"Well, I guess I can get at probably all of it."

Homer nodded thoughtfully. "I'd like to be able to use you as my personal secretary, Joyce, but I need someone in this office whom I can trust implicitly, and who can trust me. Do you understand what I am saying?"

Joyce stared at him, her eyes wide, her heart beating wildly. "He knows," her mind screamed fearfully at her. "Somehow he knows!" Now she would be fired, and—

"Do you have something you'd like to tell me?"

The young secretary stared at the new regional representative, and for the first time she truly saw the grief in Homer Bean's eyes for the death of a man who had tried to cheat him at every turn of his life. She saw too the compassion and concern Homer Bean felt for her, and suddenly she realized what that unusual something was that she had been seeing and feeling each time she had been in Homer Bean's presence.

Love! That was what he had! He was filled with pure love for other people! He did not condemn, he did not manipulate, he did not abuse his power.

125

"Mr. Bean," she said, and tears started from her eyes as she spoke, "I know I'll be fired for this, but, well, I don't care! I have to live with myself, and this will help! A few weeks ago I . . . I pulled out a list of your biggest clients. I gave them to . . . to . . . Oh, Mr. Bean, I am so sorry!"

Homer Bean stood and walked to where the young woman sat sobbing out her grief. Gently he took her hand and squeezed it, and when at last she lifted her mascara-streaked face, he smiled.

"Joyce," he said firmly as he handed her his handkerchief, "you are a wonderfully courageous woman, and I would be honored if you would accept the position as my personal secretary. Now about that meeting tomorrow . . ."

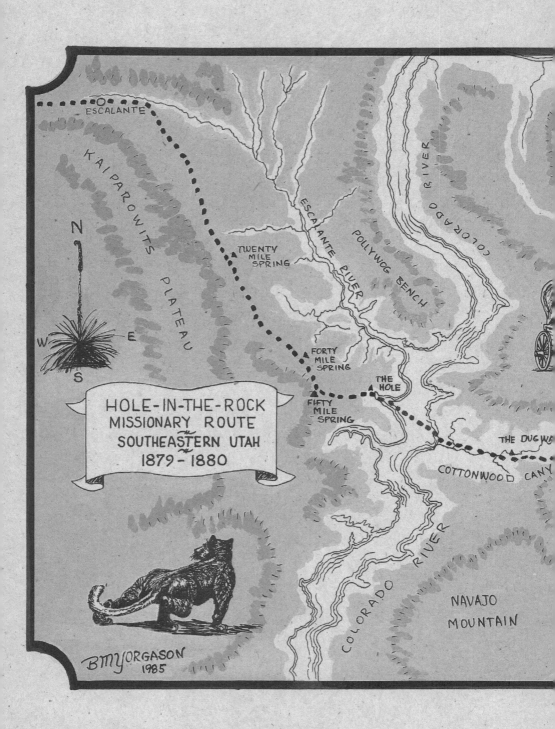

ESCALANTE

KAIPAROWITS PLATEAU

ESCALANTE RIVER

POLLYWOG BENCH

COLORADO RIVER

TWENTY MILE SPRING

N
W E
S

FORTY MILE SPRING

THE HOLE

FIFTY MILE SPRING

THE DUG WAY

COTTONWOOD CANY

HOLE-IN-THE-ROCK
MISSIONARY ROUTE
SOUTHEASTERN UTAH
1879 - 1880

COLORADO RIVER

NAVAJO
MOUNTAIN

BMYORGASON
1985